A Tourist in the Profession

A NOVEL BY

Richard Lawrance

To Christine, With Love

Email: lawrance.richard@gmail.com
ISBN: 978-0-9809575-1-1
Published: 10/2011
2nd Edition: 04/2018

Synopsis

Mei-ling Lee has returned to the Australian state of Cooksland as the first female CEO and Creative Director of the state's tourism commission, King's Company. Mei-ling pioneered cultural tourism in Australia, incorporating tourism education into a profitable tourism business, bringing new economic opportunities to regional Australia.

Head-hunted by the Singapore Tourism Commission, Mei-ling developed a similar dimension for the tourism industry in that country. After five years, the tourism chain she created – Bumiputra Chung Hindi – transformed the island nation's tourism business. She now returns to Australia to bring a new dimension of profitability to the Arts in Cooksland by linking it to the economics of cultural tourism.

Mei-ling soon finds, however, that the internal politics of the Cooksland tourism elite, combined with political machinations of the self-styled arts impresario of the newly built Cooksland Cultural Centre, Max Kingsbury, place one block after another in the way of her ambitious plan. The internecine manoeuvrings of each 'set' in Cooksland tourism's cultural landscape penetrate deep into the heart of Mei-ling's private life, threatening even the sanctity of 'home' for her partner and pre-school daughter.

In the end, the insular tourism community of Cooksland's capital, King, win; but at what cost?

Bedroom

It is early afternoon. And it is time for my daughter's nap. She is only two, but I have a video I made during our final days in Singapore, in which Rose comes up to me as I stand at the window of our eighth floor apartment, looks up into the camera and says "What are you doing?". An inquisitiveness and ability to learn that surprises me, and warns me not to take compliance with my expected order of things for granted.

Now in our ground floor apartment back home in Australia, at afternoon nap time she climbs into her cot voluntarily but sometimes unwillingly. She does not yet recognise herself as being tired. So we go through a process. I settle her down with a light cover and talk her through what she can hear. There is a large tropical treefern that grows outside her ground floor bedroom window, plus a creeper that climbs up to the veranda of the room above. So one of the first things she can hear is the breezes moving through the shadows that play on the venetian blinds beside her head. (Her cot is right next to the window. When she falls asleep, I will half close the blinds.) Breezes that tappet gently in the blade-like fronds of the treefern. Breezes in the softer, lighter green of the leaves closer to her ear. And in the wind chimes of the apartment next door.

Next she will hear the inevitable chirp or whistle of a bird somewhere nearby. Then a bus will draw away through the suburban street on which our residential apartment block is situated. Or a car will move in the distance, a truck further still. Sometimes a vessel will pass on the river frontage onto which our front door opens. A deep thud-a-chug of a silt barge as it passes up or downstream. And, on good days, we can hear children playing in a nearby primary school. Sometimes I talk to Rose about playing with them in her dreams. But mostly, we settle into silence together. My daughter and I. And eventually, Rose sleeps.

And I have that precious, precious hour in my day to myself. To sit and write. To watch the river. To fantasise. And often, against my better judgement, to get the washing up done.

*

Jalousies

I have had to wear sunglasses since we returned to Australia. The light is just too strong. Off the river. Off the concrete veranda. The whole of Australia thrown up in our faces in one brilliant sunfull. It was like that when I first arrived in this country - that sky. So blue. So big. So bright. A sun I had to shield my eyes from immediately and always have since. Britain's has always seemed so pale by comparison - one of those watery, battery-fed bantam yolks plopped onto a simpering blue wash on someone else's still wet watercolour.

Singapore's was similar - although always given body and substance by South East Asia's monsoonal immanence. As if the air was a stiff, porous sponge that gained stature and life only when it came into contact with moisture. Frail mornings anticipate a thunderous downpour at its edges. Cumulus clouds mate and mount one upon another while the sun draws across its zenith. The air quivers at the prospect of precipitation. The atmosphere becomes almost unbearable, voluptuous in its proportions. Until at last the clouds come together in great streams of liquid, gushing downwards in unmitigated deluge. The air is full and satiated. We are warm, but wet. And running for cover. Or still inside, working, grateful for the air-conditioning (even though always too cold).

Beer was the perfect beverage in Singapore. It soaked you up inside just as the air absorbed you from without, while the local food slipped and slopped around on its way down. And the

6

furniture was always vaguely damp, the walls clammy to the touch.

Australia, by comparison, is crisp and friable. Even as far north in the continent as King, the humidity seems negligible. The sun cuts through it. Searing rays shoot down, seize a dry and barren land by its edges and shake the continent firmly, regularly, so that it won't forget. Nor its inhabitants, who learn to live with it. That it will be alright when the ice caps melt and the seas rise and the loopy hothouse climate comes rushing in as they had once feared would the imagined yellow hordes from the North. Perhaps I wear the sunglasses in the hope that the sun will think I am not one of them when that time comes. A disguise. "Hey sun, look at me, I'm not one of them!" I say with a sunglassy sort of wave. Trouble is, everybody else is wearing sunglasses too.

*

Laundry

I am really glad to be 'home'. But I miss a car. Mei-ling's company has promised us one – it's in her contract - but it seems a long time coming and, in the meantime, I am pushing Rose in our Mothercare easy-fold pusher a couple of kilometres over a sizeable hill to the nearest supermarket and suburban shopping strip.

The experience is in itself culturally pleasurable. Westside is one of those dubious ethnic conglomerations that so typify multicultural Australia. An Aboriginal population who live here because it was the only bit of King the poms would allow them once the colonialists moved in on the district. The Greeks and Italians are here because housing was cheap back then and close to King's industrial zone. The Vietnamese and Cambodians are here because, as refugees, if they set up shop the Mediterraneans would buy their sort of bread. And the hippy-punk-dope-smoking-alternative-cafe-green-democrat-classless-wholefood-hydroponic-bio-organic-recycled-sustainable-environment-community-arts-pre-zeen-post-tv-cafe-latte-and-mineral-water generation moved in to live off the cuisine and groceries generated by the rest - as long as it didn't have MSG or preservatives.

Having spent five years in a relatively seamless and almost religious homogeneity of "multicultural" Singapore, this is the sort of spilling-all-over-the-saucer culture I have missed. Trouble is, it means hanging cheap, rustling plastic bags of shopping from every extremity of Rose's pusher, making sure she has something to occupy her for the trip home (preferably something wholesome, like baked pumpkin from the 'roasts' take-away joint), and making the long push back to the apartment. If I have to stop for anything or let go of the pusher for a second, the whole system overbalances. At such times I miss the taxis, trains and buses of Singapore. Or a car.

Then there is doing the laundry. To begin with it is almost a pleasure. Re-awakening practices a maid has performed for us for five years. Leisurely loading the machine, applying the powder and softener, allowing crude mechanics to swish away while Rose and I amuse ourselves in the dim vault of car parking bay under our sweaty, sixties concrete block of medium-to-long-term apartments. Then wheeling it out lazily to the wonderfully Australian Hills Hoist, underneath giant, generous Moreton Bay figs, in amongst hibiscus and frangipani. A great sense of being Australian again.

But after a while, Rose starts to get bored. And I all too quickly exhaust my supply of games and songs, and so we take even longer, looking for distractions along the way. And need to find other things to do that will nevertheless last only the length of the washing cycle. And Rose will find more distractions on the way back, or simply stop in the middle of the path, in the hope it seems that I would somehow change my mind. And so the laundry has us as an extension of its own action, arcing this way and that, vacillating and evacuating, flushing in and out of the apartment, in an effort to get things clean and/or done. If there is any single factor that motivates me to get us out of here and into a home of our own, it has become the laundry. That and the need to feel settled enough to get stuck into my thesis.

*

Foundation

Proposal Draft.

The cultural tourism movement of the 1980s proposed a radical revision of the traditional business model for tourism. The tradition of tourism that emerged from the Second World War saw a return to the pre-war emphasis on tourism by the wealthier classes out of the country of domicile to places deemed *exotic*.

For the British, this may have been as geographically close as the South of France or Spain. For Americans, it might have involved Europe in general, but also began to include Pacific venues such as Hawaii. For Australians, however, the focus remained primarily the UK and, perhaps, northern Europe. The Mediterranean was seen as the source of a second class migrant population that was 'invading' Australia and 'taking our jobs' – although in reality most of the jobs taken by the post-war wave of migrants were new, resulting from planned economic expansion in the manufacturing sector designed for their labour.

Although Australians in the 1950s and 60s were exposed to South East Asia and the Pacific region through popular culture – musicals such as *South Pacific* and films such as the James Bond series – it did not assume a focus for tourism. It was not until the emergence of the backpacker phenomenon in the late 60s that destinations such as Bali began to feature on the tourism horizon, and even then this was seen as 'adventure' tourism or 'hippy' tourism. The cultural attractions of India, Indonesia, Singapore, Malaysia, Thailand and Hong Kong did not become a marketing currency for Australian tourism until the 1970s. It was also during the 1970s that Australia began to understand it might itself become a tourist destination for its near region – particularly for the Japanese.

Generic promotional campaigns like the famous "prawn on the barbi" resulted directly from an identification of Australian cultural characteristics that could generically be used to promote Australia as a tourist destination. It was the cultural tourism movement of the 1980s that began to identify cultural activity within Australia as worth promoting not only to international visitors but also for the domestic market. This began with specific events in discrete destinations, in which 'cultural' events were developed to intensify market appeal. The "music in the vineyard" phenomenon is one strong example of a trend that had a measurable impact in the domestic market as well as overseas. State arts festivals, with associated fringe festivals, were similarly supported by government in the 1980s primarily for their tourist dollar potential.

One of the keys to the longer-term sustainability of the cultural tourism movement, however, was the involvement of local volunteerism. Towns and regions in rural Australia in particular were supported in identifying one local cultural event that could be developed to a level to attract and provide real service satisfaction for domestic and international visitors. The application of community development principles to regional and local tourism by exponents of cultural tourism led further, to an integration of tourism into the Australian economy as a major economic driver. Tourism became a major contributor to regional growth around the country, as well as a significant indicator of national economic health. The role of the cultural tourism movement in rural Australia, for instance, in ensuring survival of the local agricultural show is well documented (reference).

The Surrey Street Travel Company is well documented elsewhere (references) as a pioneer in the cultural tourism movement of the 1980s. It secured the first federal government grants from the newly formed Tourism Australia Council (TAC) to take 'tourism education' into Sydney schools. Drawing on examples from the performing arts industry, Surrey Street developed interactive performance-based experiences for young people which introduced them not only to cultural experiences outside Australia, but also those within Australia. The educational aim of the program was to develop a service mentality, based on the principle that for cultural tourism to sustain and build on its economic viability, the development throughout the Australian community of a culture of service to tourists was necessary.

The success of the Surrey Street in-schools program was reflected in its financial outcomes, as even state schools willingly purchased its activities. The program became independent of government subsidy within three years. Based on this success, Surrey Street persuaded the TAC to fund a more ambitious performance-based cultural tourism extravaganza at the Sydney Entertainment Centre. Again, this showcase drew on the performing arts traditions for its structure and production values, using spectacular design, sets, lighting, live music and performance to introduce the public to South East Asian cultures in a meeting with Australian culture, in a way that firmly communicated the 'culture of service' message. Again, box office returns alone demonstrated the economic viability of the model.

The Creative Associate at Surrey Street responsible for these initiatives, Mei-ling Lee, was subsequently offered a position by the Singapore Tourism Authority. Singapore was already more aware of the link between tourism and local economy, and the need for a culture of service, than Australia (substantiate this). Lee was given (language) a middle weight suite of retail outlets to mould into a Surrey Street style new program. The resulting company, Bahasa Huayu Tamil (BHT), succeeded over a five year period in delivering:

• a measurable impact on Singapore out-tourism to South and South East Asia (including Australia)

• a well documented sharpening of the 'brand identification' of Singapore's various cultural 'markets', and

• a measurable increase in visitor satisfaction exit surveys in relation to the cultural and service experiences.

Although no correlation was established between the BHT enterprise and in-tourism, the number of visitor days in Singapore increased substantially and consistently over the five year period of Mei-ling Lee's directorship of Bahasa Huaya Tamil.

Lee has now returned to Australia to assume a position with the Cooksland state government's tourism commission, King's Company. Lee is the first female to assume the joint position of Creative Director and Chief Executive Officer of a state tourism commission in Australia. Her brief is to apply her experience from Singapore to Cooksland, and utilise the cultural tourism praxis she has developed to integrate King's Company into the state's new cultural centre on the King River in King, the capital of Cooksland.

Cooksland is the first state in Australia to attempt this integration of state cultural activity – including museums, art gallery and performing arts centre – into its tourism economy. It is seen as a major shift not only in tourism policy but also in arts policy. It is expected that major economic viability benefits will flow to an arts industry that is, in Australia, traditionally dependent on government subsidy.

Lee also aims, however, to bring to King's Company a management style and ethos that reflects the principles of cultural tourism. This entails the implementation of a management model that is developmental, based on community development practices. The leadership style will be transformational rather than transactional or charismatic. Management will involve a flat structure led by an executive management team which will base its decision-making style on consensus and supported direction, rather than traditional top-down hierarchic management models.

In this thesis, the author proposes to draw on cultural, sociological, management and organisational theory to track the implementation of Mei-ling Lee's management model at King's Company. The action research question proposed by the author is: is the viability of a service-based business organisation enhanced by a management-led organisational culture that reflects the culture of the product?

Notes: the product is the service – this needs to be clearer. + too long, too much history – this is more like an introduction.

*

Demography

I find it hard getting my head around the tourism politics here. It's as if we are being courted - invited to one dinner party or garden party or barbecue after another. And what I find, coming in as an outsider, is a highly observable landscape of factions, each one of which wants us to become part of their 'set', rather than of all the other 'sets'. Interestingly, each faction represents a particular historical cohort of tourism in Cooksland. They even live physically in the same suburbs. But the history of the suburbs themselves does not always necessarily match, which disrupts the metaphor.

Take the old 'colonialists', for instance. Arte de Leon is the first cab off the rank. He has us over almost the minute we get off the plane. He inhabits that early twentieth century Eurocentric tourism tradition of cruises and 'tours'. Hails from the era that 'invented' tourism, when 'tours' were led by a 'tour director', whom everybody on the tour just 'adored' for his flair and panache, exquisite choice of accommodation or restaurant etc.

Everything else in the industry is disdained by the de Leon's of the world as just 'retail travel'. He studied under noted cruise impresarios in London and was a Cruise Director with the National Line over there on minor routes. Returned from the motherland with his fine voice and eloquent style to become lord of the fledgling Cooksland Tourism Company, which secured enough investment to employ some *creative personnel*, as he refers to them (and, by dint I assume, himself). Even then, de Leon scores only the occasional international cruise for CTC, and has to *stoop* to organising CTC's first tours into SE Asia and the Pacific. It is just *so* demeaning, it seems. Essentially, however, De Leon is a director of the CTC in the more bureaucratic sense of state government qangos. The actual and inaugural Creative Director of CTC was an Englishman, Edward Alleyn. He is already well-versed in the use of creative personnel in tour and tourism campaign design, and overlooks De Leon to draw most of his leading creative staff from 'down south' and overseas.

De Leon is, however, surrounded by legions of cruise and tour devotees who dutifully write letters to the papers singing his praises. They turn up at all of his launches and gloath about 'De Leon tours' afterwards. They thrill for an invitation to his frequent and lavish dinner parties and luncheons, and fervently support his regular assaults in the press against the 'interloper' from interstate who replaces Alleyn, Tristan Malthorpe – especially when Malthorpe changes the name of the CTC to King's Company in a move to reflect that absurdly parochial and vanity-ridden trend of naming state tourism authorities after the capital cities in which they are based..

Anyway, after successfully making Malthorpe's stay in King as miserable in the media as he can, Arte de Leon duly applies for the job of Creative Director of King's Company when it comes up. Unfortunately, it is Mei-ling who gets the job. So Arte invites us over for a barbecue (not the lavish dinner, note), to meet some of the local 'professionals'.

At de Leon's we also meet Byron Wetherall, another local exponent of the Eurocentric colonialist tradition, who lives "just a couple of streets away" from de Leon. Wetherall made his fame in Australia, rather than "overseas", with minor creative roles in state tourism commission tours and cruises, and early offshore tourism television - enough to fuel the notion that he is 'established' national tour and cruise material (well, near as). He never sank so low, however, as to involve himself in the regional vagaries of the cultural tourism movement of the 1980s. He has 'standards'.

He too has had irregular and secondary appointments with the Cooksland Tourism Company. Malthorpe goes to great lengths to woo him during his time, but while Wetherall seems compliant on the surface, he is as venal as de Leon behind the scenes. Mei-ling has already been warned. He is reputedly responsible for a stream of venomous, anonymous faxes that followed her appointment. Mostly these attacked the Commission (King's Company's governance body) for not supporting local professionals, but they also vilified Mei-ling as a lesbian, particularly in her choice of Phillipa Hay as general manager. The Chair apparently confronted Wetherall directly, told him he would never work in King again if the campaign did not stop. Wetherall, needless to say, had also applied for the job Mei-ling got. And here he is at de Leon's barbi, smiling and beaming away at us, cooing over Rose.

The colonialists, including Edward Alleyn (now happily retired here), all live in post-federation villas of the Art Nouveau era. Perfect! Mei-ling has offered both de Leon and Wetherall leadership roles in her first year of activity. De Leon, several. Keep them in the fold and out of the papers – that's the plan, anyway. After Singapore, I find it hard to imagine how tourism gossip can be so 'big' in the King media.

We also meet Lillith Plant at De Leon's, another local aficionado Mei-ling has been alerted to. But Lillith is not on her usual cultural patch. She promptly invites us to a dinner party at her place. And there we meet an entirely different set who, like Lillith, acquired their knowledge of and interest in tourism at the tertiary level. These are graduates of the old university – the sandstone stock who went on to teaching positions in the tourism courses established by the new universities that grew out of the Colleges of Advanced Education. They were brought up on SE Asian tourism opportunities, ticket discounting, deregulation of the airlines, mass retail travel agencies, retail branding, customised round-the-world packages and the like. They understood cultural tourism in its seminal form, and are a product of the computer age, although not the internet. The De Leons and Wetheralls of the old cruise and tour tradition are to them like stone gargoyles of a colonial past.

Like the De Leons and Wetheralls, however, they too have had to satisfy their early professional ambitions in university-based travel agencies and emerging corporates, with only occasional bites at the well-resourced state government CTC run by Alleyn and, later, Malthorpe. And all the while secretly, at private dinner parties, they dream of institutionalising a revolutionary future for Australian tourism led by the north, by the creative flair of Cooksland tourism professionals.

Lillith seems to want us to embrace a histrionic scenario of neglect by the CTC/Kings Company. She and her colleagues are the true foundation of a professional future in Cooksland. And since one of her friends, Daphne Barnsworth, is on King's Company's governance Commission, Mei-ling sensibly offers her a creative slot in the first year's promotional program as well as a role developing a major cultural tourism event.

By rights, Lillith's cohort should inhabit bright modern 1960s architecture, but they stray from the mould. Their part of town is more 1930s and 40s – Deco and pre-war, bungalows mostly. Or the style on stilts they call Cookslanders.

Then there is the gay set. They return to historicity: all vituperatively postmodernist, and inhabit either the gross 'council estate' 60s flats, in some sort of post-structuralist protest, or the more modern apartments retrofitted into gentrified working class suburbs. They fancy their intellect's intersection with sexual exclusiveness, sensibility, and the affective realm of ideas places them alone in the centre of the street, forbidding entry by strength of mere presence. Their 'suburb' will detach and blast its own highway into the future of the global tourism. Tourism of the future, they believe, will be via the internet – no, not e-sales of live tours, but e-tourism – vision and text and intercultural simulation that individuals purchase around the globe in the desperate darkness of their midnight bedsits, all cut and paste and manufactured in the home-based computer networks of Kendall Chamberlain, Nimrod Hannah and their kind.

They only invite us to coffee shops, in suburbs other than their own (most notably our own Westside, meeting on our 'ground'). Their conversations, like their lives, mount a post-structuralist assault on just about any topic, and their tourism practice sets impossible new parameters that only they understand.

But many influential bureaucrats in government live amongst them, and they also run said coffee shops, and the alternative press and media. They have a control over the chat rooms and minor news sheets in which the real exchange of ideas that drives King's cultural streetscape takes place, completely outside the orbit of the mainstream newspapers and tv stations who think they have local thought sewn up. They truly understand what it is to 're-colonise' the streetscape. And they also get funding from Tourism Australia. Malthorpe used their leading designer, Kendall Chamberlain, in his first major live promotions, and Mei-ling has offered Chamberlain and their leading nearest postmodern semblance of a creative director, Nimrod Hannah, a major role in developing e-tourism and virtual tourism components to her inaugural program, including the live computer-assisted promotions in King's prestigious new Performance Centre.

So these are the invites. But Mei-ling also elects to stride boldly into two new 'suburbs' of her own choosing. Firstly, she has offered employment to the inhabitants of yet another quarter of King's tourism culture – those who are currently re-populating the working class suburbs around the new Cooksland University of Technology's cultural tourism degree course - the young graduates. This group have no geographical demographic yet. They are still finding their way, applying for cultural tourism grants, or gaining experience with the Lilith Plants of King. But Mei-ling believes she must bring them together, because they, as she once was, really ARE the future of the industry. And the only way to balance the current whirligig of competing interests is to develop a creative workforce from a new axis.

That and continue to bring in the counterweight 'heavies' from interstate, in the tradition of Alleyn and Malthorpe. She thus also contracts some of Australia's leading tourism directors and promotion designers, including Tristan Malthorpe himself, in a program of tourism activity visibly of the local and of the best from across the country, in which she humbly gives herself only one live promotion slot right at the very end of the year.

And finally, she has entered the alternative shop-front tourism emerging in King's disadvantaged fringe. This is Mei-ling's most risk-laden investment, and it is the one that most excites her. One of the developments of the cultural tourism movement she did so much to initiate during the 80s has been a generation of school children from socially disadvantaged and marginalised groups in the community who have thought: why can't this be for us too? If it worked for rural Australia, why can't it work for us? And so the educational thrust of the Surrey Streets around Australia has started to do what culture does best: transfer itself to the next generation.

Dale Balanda's Cult Tourism is a small-scale outer-urban business which acts as a magnet for the new graduates, but also for older alternative tourist operators from the old community-based cultural tourism movement, who value the mobilising capacity of cultural tourism for the masses and the minorities.

Dale and his partner, Robert, are relatively new in town and, although gay, not yet integrated into any of the local tourism factions. They are both, however, representing "youth" on the national Tourism Australia Council. Mei-ling hopes that it is this disenfranchised but burgeoning feature of the King tourism streetscape that will form the vanguard of her new axis.

Dale and Robert actually come to 'our house', rather than invite us to theirs. Phillipa brings them round one Sunday afternoon, and we share a bottle of wine. Robert jokes he has heard there is already a book out on how long Mei-ling will last in King, given the various factions and their unconcealed ambitions. I asked him what the odds were. He said six months. Phillipa smiles.

She can have a wicked smile, Phillipa. There is a real glint right at the outward corners of her deep brown eyes, as her laugh lines crease up in what can often be an impassive, richly featured face. This smile has the same glint as the one she flashed in our hotel room, during our first visit to King as a family, when Mei-ling came down during her closing weeks with BHT for some initial business planning. Talked about old Surrey Street days. And she and I of days back at uni, when we studied journalism together - before she bottled it, I reminded her, and plumped for the safer marketing course. And there was the smile, for a moment. And then Mei-ling started to talk to her about her plans for King's Company, and the management structure and approach she wanted. And the smile came again broadening, as if she knew what was coming next. And when Mei-ling asked if her she was interested in joining the management team, the glint came into the eye. Yes, she said, she had been wondering the same thing. It would be an opportunity not to be missed. She was becoming bored with the Department of Tourism anyway. Too bureaucratic... by which time we were all smiling.

Sometimes it's just nice to have friends, I guess.

*

House

Well, we have finally settled into our own house. I feel awkward being the driving factor here. I know Mei-ling should come first. And so should Rose. I wanted to be in this role. I wanted to be the support-person and primary care-giver. Mei-ling is the first woman in Australia to get a state tourism commission. I'm happy that her career is the one that 'carries' us. Theoretically, now that she is established in the role, she should be off on some world tour over the Christmas period sussing out destination options. But I want us to be settled in a home of our own for our first Christmas back in Australia. I want us to have some time together at a time of year that, for me, is about being with those you love. It's a sentimental driver, I know, servicing a need of mine. But it's also a landmark I want to reach in order to mark off a period called 'arrival' and put it behind me. I need to be able to orient myself somehow, instead of feeling transitory.

I also want Rose to be 'settled in' too. This is the first Christmas she will fully comprehend, even if only for the presents. I want it to be in our own home, with our furniture and a hi-fi I can play Christmas music on, with some of the Singapore we have recently left spread around us a bit. And, I have to admit, I also want my own office back – I need my books, my desk, my computer. I can't relinquish that sense of my own professional future, even if it is only a yet-to-be-attained qualification at this stage. Mei-ling has an office elsewhere, but for me there is still that promised time when Rose has her nap that I am yet to utilise to best effect.

It's ironic the house we have bought is one of the first we looked at. I liked it from the start. Old weatherboard, typical of the region

– on the high side of the street, tall stumps that provide plenty of air underneath and room for an open laundry. Built on the cross to make the most of those vital breezes in summer. Verandas front and back. Off-street parking. Modest back garden. Situated well back on the block. But Mei-ling needed to go through almost two months of So you're from Singapore Well This property is close to such-and-such private hospital and That business centre and an excellent medical centre close by – 24 hours service, banking facilities, Shopping centre just down the road, Deli just on the next corner (but not the corner of *your* street), Close to these sporting facilities or That entertainment complex, swimming pool just around the corner – but nobody ever parks in *this* street, quiet neighbours but there if you need them, Catholic School just minutes' drive. High return investment area here, only three minutes from the city, only five minutes from the city, only seven minutes from the city, only ten minutes from the city but so much more space, fifteen but *excellent* transport services – bus, train and, of course, the ferry along the river – they are introducing a *jetcat* soon! (You don't always want to be taking the car in, do you?) - before we turned up back here. Full circle. She didn't even remember it from the first visit. I tried not to remind her. And she said yes.

I can't help feeling pressed between a quiet satisfaction and self-recrimination. But I still sit here on the veranda, gazing out across a gentle dell of suburb, just over a rise from the city but we could be out in the bush for all quiet of it, and the lovely Victorian architecture of King's Grammar inscribing the heat haze on the horizon. Smug bastard? Not pleasant. And there, nemesis: Rose calls.

*

Walls

I thought I would get over the 'walls' thing once we were back in Australia. In Singapore, it was because I could only drink within the confines of our home. Gin and tonics while I was cooking. A bottle of wine with the meal. Something as a night cap – probably cognac – which extended into the bottle if our discussion of Mei-ling's work went on into the night.

Singapore's multiculturalism seems such a knocked-together-with-nails affair in retrospect – there on the surface and in the letter of government policy, but it's not far beneath that each ethnic group – the Indians, Malays, Chinese and, of course, Westerners –disappear from the official intercourse into their own cultural enclaves. Bahasa Huayu Tamil employed a couple of nominal Indians and Malays, but it was predominantly Chinese. I hated being singled out a western male because I drank alcohol. I know it was a face-giving exercise, but it was so obvious nobody else was being asked. And I always had to say yes, to give face back. But only the one drink.

Mei-ling, even though she was a 'banana skin', seemed to take to it. She became a more consummate tea drinker than the BHTers. And I suppose my ego quite liked the surface semblance of respect. But it just meant that inside our home, just as the walls of our apartment seeped with the humidity of the climate outside, so inside them my mind was soused and immured from the tensions infusing my brain. Being a foreigner. Being an outsider. Being beyond the usually attributed place for males. Alcohol was the only site into which I could totally immerse myself and not feel threatened.

This is not true, of course. Rose transformed my life. From the moment her head rose above the hygiene barrier and her little face screwed up and yelled for all it was worth at the shock of this necessary but horrifying air, and they put her onto Mei-ling's breast, Mei-ling's eyes just awash with joy, I knew I would never be the same again. I felt I could do anything. Been up for 24 hours, but still went back to the apartment and made all the necessary calls to folks back home through the woolly fog of elation. I even went into a church the next day, just to sit still and be thankful. It felt so good to be a father. I had thought loving Mei-ling had been all I could wish for, but the upwelling of feeling with Rose was unimaginable. I wanted everything for her. Couldn't believe the expanse of emotional landscape that opened out within me, across which I ranged in every direction and all at once with my hope for Rose and her future.

And then Rose took us outside the walls of our home. Wherever we went with her in Singapore, she was welcomed. And that meant we were welcomed. A baby, I found, gave us instant currency with others, regardless of ethnic background and language barriers. Rose created a social ease for us in public that helped me understand just how hard I had found the insulation of living in another culture (let alone another triad of cultures). How dependent I had become on the privacy afforded by the walls of our apartment for my personal survival as a self.

It is thus frustrating to me that, now we are here once more in a home we own (or are buying), with our thin weatherboard walls close to the outside air, to the ground, and to the more familiar suburban streetscape, I have come once more dependent on the walls. For now Mei-ling's official position demands exactly the same sobriety wherever we go. Alcohol is still something I can afford to consume only within the confines of our own house. For whenever we go out, we are dealing with yet another quadrant of King's factionalised tourism community. Every dinner is political. The only place Mei-ling and I actually get to relax together is at home.

I expected to be so 'free' back 'home' in Australia. I expected to be anonymous, a denizen once more. And even with Rose now I am just one of any number of parents on the street. Rose still means the world to us, but we are like every other English-speaking parent here to whom their infant is everything. We are just part of the sociology, and our walls are all that protect us from it.

*

Home

Well, Mei-ling had representatives of every tourism 'suburb' in the streetscape over to 'her house' today. They all came in their finery – Arte De Leon, Byron Wetherall, Lillith Plant, Daphne Barnsworth, Nimrod Hannah and Kendall Chamberlain, Dale and Robert – all from their various factional enclaves to the new South Bank premises of King's Company, in the cultural as well as the tourism heart of King, for the official launch of Mei-ling's strategic vision for Cooksland tourism, and her first year's program of activity.

In the light and airy function room on the river that is the centrepiece of the King's Company office, a string quartet played to a champagne breakfast, and local politicians mingled with members of the company's governing Commission and the rich geography of King's tourist industry. It was a truly eclectic event. She is very clever, my Mei-ling. She knows the pundits are predicting she will be run out of town within six months. With luck, she's given herself at least a 12 month start.

It is unlikely that the entire membership of the Cooksland tourism elite, and not-so-elite, have ever before been brought together in the same room, to celebrate a future in which they all have a role. De Leon looked uncomfortably pompous – and why wouldn't you with a name like that? - ostentatiously sporting a cigarette in a long holder, that he was obviously not allowed to light during the launch. (Although later he made a point of taking the Minister for Tourism and the Arts, Douglas Dingwall, out onto the veranda for a 'private audience', in order to light up.)

Wetherall, the shorter of the two, beamed hypocritically beside him, make the two look like an inverse Laurel and Hardy – one buffoon tall and effete, the other short and plump. Wetherall even beamed when the Chairman of the King's Company Commission, Derek Barrimore, went over to shake his hand in welcome. Barrimore's face was as impassive as I imagine it was when he threatened to run Wetherall out of town if he did not cease his vicious anonymous fax campaign against Mei-ling's appointment. But if Wetherall registered the disapprobation, no-one would have known it for the champagne smarm smeared across his jovial face.

Lillith Plant looked nervously 'at home' – as if she felt she had a right to be there, thought that on principle she ought not to be, but was privately hopeful that she was glad that she was. Beside her, Daphne Barnsworth positively bustled, introducing Plant to other Commissioners and the occasional parliamentary back bencher.

Hannah and Chamberlain held themselves apart, finger-clapped politely at Mei-ling's speech and the Minister's reply, and talked earnestly to each other over barely sipped flutes of champagne, until Dale and Robert interrupted them whilst doing the rounds. These two they greeted like longed-for friends, with smiles and effusively limp handshakes. Nimrod and Robert even exchanged cheek-to-cheek kissy-kisses. It was terribly gay. But as soon as the pair moved on, it was back to the earnest behind-hand conversation and self-imposed isolation.

Dale and Robert both worked the room, clearly conscious that this was their official introduction too, and aware that it was Mei-ling who had created the opportunity for them.

There was one group, however, who were painfully present by their absence: King's arts community. Even though the Minister referred, in his speech, to the visionary and historic decision to house Kings Company here with Mei-ling's appointment, in the same building precinct as the Museum, the Art Gallery, and the Performance Centre just across the road. Even though he re-iterated Mei-ling's bold brief to bring the arts centre-stage in a grand cultural vision for the development of tourism in Cooksland and, perhaps, Australia, whereby the arts could learn from the financial independence of the tourist industry.

Even though he applauded the vision of King's Company, the state's tourism commission, in 'head-hunting' this innovative young industry leader from her pioneering work in South East Asia – a decision which the state government was one hundred percent behind – the Minister had been unable to convince the CEO of the Performance Centre and self-appointed kingmaker of Cooksland's limited performing arts scene, Maxwell Kingsbury, to attend the launch. Nor any of the performing artists who depended on Kingsbury for performance space and programming opportunities.

Prestigious real estate situated on the banks of the King River, the Performance Centre is still incomplete. It joins the new museum and art gallery (in which King's Company's offices are housed) to form the cultural centre of the burgeoning city. And one of its venues, the Next Stage, is supposed to be under construction for the sole use King's Company. Mei-ling's specific brief is to work with Kingbury to use the proven box-office power of cultural tourism extravaganzas to subsidise the activity of the performing arts, particularly King's languishing theatre industry.

The Minister's comment today is meant to demonstrate the extent to which Cooksland state government policy is underwriting the bold strategy enunciated by Mei-ling at her interview: to directly sub-contract King's performance arts exponents to design and present King's Company cultural tourism promotions, and to place performing arts events at the centre of Cooksland's cultural tourism agenda. Mei-ling's promise to government is that she will not only directly cross-subsidise the arts with her own tourism promotional activity, but place the arts on a footing as cultural tourism in its own right. Box office will replace government subsidy as the key to viability for the arts, as it is for cultural tourism.

This is a torchsong step for the state government. It signifies the rolling of arts policy into tourism policy. Traditionally, a theatre would be given to a performing arts company, but such is government's commitment to cultural tourism as a solution to arts industry viability, it is turning this venue over to King's Company in its entirety.

At least, that is the promise in public, and Mei-ling's own understanding on accepting her position. But Max Kingsbury is playing hard-to-get. No invitation. No meetings. No attendance at the program launch. All roads, it seems, must lead to Max. Even Mei-ling's. For Max is a capital investment by the government itself; Max is the high rise of King's culture 'currently under construction'. Max has to be seen to be worth the money when the voters go to the polls. And for Max, the money is in traditional performing arts fare. And if Mei-ling is here to change all of that, then Max, for Mei-ling, is going to be hard work.

The symbolism of today's launch cannot be lost on anyone in attendance. Even the local dance and theatre companies, all heavily subsidised by the state, only sent their marketing officers.

I was glad I had Rose to occupy my attention. And to provide a welcome relief for Mei-ling.

As for Mei-ling herself, what followed the launch perhaps best illustrates where the incoming CEO of King's Company resides in Kings cultural tourism map. For while she succeeded in drawing them all out of their respective suburbs to attend launch of her inaugural program, and her strategic plan for the future was well received and judged sound, the denizens returned to their native haunts; whereas Mei-ling comes home with Rose and myself to our new home, and the cake and snacks I have pulled together with my own fair hands (mostly out of a packet, I confess). And with our old friend Phillipa Hay, our new friends Dale Balanda and Robert Cunningham, and a glass of champagne, overlooking our new miniature rain forest of a back yard, we celebrate our daughter's first birthday back in Australia. It is still good to be home. Even if 'home' itself remains a little weird.

*

Transport 1

The car has finally arrived – a full three months after we had. All the fuss in the first few weeks about choosing a model and getting the order into government (King's Company gets their vehicles through government purchase), in the end we didn't get our vehicle of choice and it has taken forever to materialise. It didn't matter so much over the Christmas period because we had Phillipa's while she went off bush-bashing, so we were able to get around to gather goodies over the break. But now Mei-ling is back into the swing of it. And of course everything is important. First ever cultural tourism promotion in the Performance Centre coming up. So Mei-ling is finding all of the face-giving ways she can of looking over people's shoulders, making sure the production side of things is absolutely spot on so that the artistic team can relax into it. For Mei-ling, then, the arrival of the car is simply a release from her dependence on taxis in the morning.

We have never talked this through, but the unspoken assumption has always been, I suppose, that I would drive Mei-ling in and pick her up so that Rose and I could have the vehicle during the day. Mei-ling likes to be driven places. She likes to be picked up at the end of the day. And I know that if she isn't, she will simply stay at work. She is not well known for her capacity to stop work, any more than she is for her ability to be on time. Always late. Always going over time. Notices others looking at their watches before she becomes aware that she is herself hungry or thirsty. Even during coffee breaks, she continues working – talking to admin or production staff, making managerial decisions on other projects or tenders or campaigns with administrative, PR and education officers.

That had been easier to do with BHT – they were all workaholics in Singapore. Not so here. Here there are unions and procedures and protocols and unspoken "ways of doing things". King is really little more than an expansive provincial country town. And I think it has come as a shock to Mei-ling to be reminded just how resistant to 'work' Australian workers can be, particularly on the performance side. There is such a self-consciousness bound up with the ontology of 'worker'; as if it is sacrosanct as a point of being, locked into 'rights' as much as functionality, something one 'is' before it 'does'.

With Surrey Street, they were all working as a team, and tourism is dollar-driven. But in the brand spanking new Performance Centre, everything is in its own government subsidised time. No unnecessary risks. In Singapore we created a memory of professionalism "back home" that, we are quickly realising, might never actually have existed.

So Mei-ling's insistence on being driven to work *on time* is both surprising and understandable. It certainly took me by surprise. I was still in my bathrobe, and Rose settling down to watch *Sesame Street*. I was making her some breakfast. And there is Mei-ling furiously ironing her clothes – something she usually leaves for me to do while she has a cup of tea and slice of toast. And next there she is, bag in hand, moving through the house. "Come on, I've got to be there." It was only 8.45am.

So I was angry that I hadn't been forewarned. Where was the communication of this new imperative? I had to quickly shuffle my body into clothes, while Rose came as she was, wrapped up in a shawl. It was a tense journey. I mean, I understand that Mei-ling is the breadwinner. Rose and I are the family at home. Mei-ling is the commuter, and the result of her commuting is what pays the bills. She was going *into* work, to appointments and budgets and arrangements and meetings and projects and initiatives and multiple demands upon her time. We battle our way in with other commuters, our vehicle metaphysically barging others out of the way, racing lights and intersections, risking the bodywork in the chariot race to work.

For Mei-ling, this is the beginning of a pace that runs her day. For Rose and I, it is a brief intervention. For the rest of our time, Rose and I lead another life – at a pace at which Rose wants to do things, or *can* do things, in counterpoint with the order and manner in which tasks present themselves to me from the house.

I begin to understand what it feels like to be a housewife.

*

Budget

Shopping complexes have become something a feature of the landscape in contemporary Australia. Like urban mountains, complete with internal cave systems. You can still go to larger country towns and find high streets – lines of shops and stores along a main street frequented by all. In high streets you meet people in passing, have casual conversations in ones and twos, aware of the impediment you represent to pedestrian traffic. Community is a series of casual encounters in which you arrange to meet later with more people in more accommodating spaces elsewhere.

But even in most sizeable country towns these days, there is a supermarket complex behind the high street. And in the cities, supermarket complexes have expanded to become shopping precincts so large that you can literally lose yourself in them, not remember where you parked the car, not know which entrance you came in or how to get out to the street you need.

They are a world in themselves, and require intimate knowledge to understand their geography and culture. You can usually eat there, go to the movies there, leave the kids in child care there. In fact, they are so large that their managers arrange community events within them. Acts promoting products, chintzy entertainment for kids bought on the cheap, fashion shows, and promotion for approvable community action like Daffodil Day for cancer research, Red Nose Day for cot death, Remembrance Day for war veterans support, the Lions, the Rotary, the Country Women's Association, the Red Cross.

Amnesty International doesn't get much of a look-in. The Unemployed Worker's Union has to hire a rundown shopfront on the now disused high street. The youth workers and social workers have to do the same. Second-hand clothes and household goods shops run by welfare organisations for the poor and socially disenfranchised are relegated to the vestige of a commercial and community past. They are not admitted to the new world of retail bliss. Social capital, it seems, is a currency in theory only. The new community is economic. Culture is the transmission of spending practices.

I was discussing this today with Robert, who I happened across in our nearest. Like Mei-ling, Dale was working. Robert just seemed to be wandering around, window shopping, and was happy to accompany Rose and myself for a while. He was great with her. Actually talked to her, at her level. And seemed to switch easily with me from 'shopping' talk to a higher level of analysis. We both found the subject of the consumer economy highly amusing.

He wanted to know how I was finding Australia after a time away, and I reflected on a realisation that returning to an urban geography I have never really been familiar with, having always lived in the inner city ring, these shopping complexes were more like bunkers – large and forbidding fortresses in the landscape that squat there, expansive and brooding. Like giant rectangular inanimate chooks sitting on eggs. Now we have a car, I have to find and locate them in order to find cheaper shopping. And once I find them, I have to find my way around them, in such a way that the experience is also meaningful and engaging for Rose.

I think this is because the urban landscape in Australia is so often so flat. Single-storey houses are the norm, and they proliferate endlessly across squares, rectangles and curves such that the larger institutions – hospitals, shopping complexes, the CBD – all stand out. In Singapore the whole island was above ground. We all lived in apartment blocks, and these seemed to connect themselves to shopping complexes in similar multi-storey buildings imperceptibly. Sure, the high rise in the CBD was bigger than that in the suburbs, and the hotels and shopping complexes stood out architecturally, but basically you moved from one to the other with ease. All part of the same geology, as it were. You were never out of 'the city' – except when you went to Sentosa Island for 'recreation', and the 'construction' of 'recreation' made even that 'escape' of dubious credibility.

Robert was familiar with Singapore. He reminded me how easy shopping in Singapore was. Westerners have plenty of money to spend and there is plenty of quality to buy at affordable prices. And locals there tend to treat shopping itself as recreation – what else is there to do in time off work but spend the money you have earnt? But back in Australia, Mei-ling's income has halved. And we are buying a house. And I am suddenly acutely aware that, even though Mei-ling is in one of the country's top jobs in her profession, and being paid accordingly, we have to budget.

I'd never had to do this before. When it was just me, or even just Mei-ling and me, I'd always just bought what we could afford. And we ate out as we could. But now that I have to radically reduce my spending practices, I have to think about it ahead, organise. When could we buy this item, how would we save up for these essential purchases for Rose. What could we afford and when in terms of renovations within the house, and additions to it. Where is the line across which we are over-capitalising the property?

I stopped short of revealing this to Robert. I began to realise I was already telling him too much. In reality, I returned home to an Excel spreadsheet I have opened up to plan and track our domestic budget, projected costs and spending, like a profit-and-loss balance sheet. I find, impossibly, that even though the spreadsheet continues to turn out a factual reality that we are living beyond our means, and cannot afford to live on Mei-ling's wage – this is based on *actual* expenditure – we actually get by each week. I keep going over and over the figures, and work the

Excel, and we always come out in the red on the paper but not in reality. I look to chaos theory in vain.

In the end I have given in, as Mei-ling had been urging me to from the beginning. I haven't stopped worrying about the money, but I have quarantined in a smaller part of my consciousness the obsessive action of our budget's impossibility. I have settled into the habit of going to the most comfortable shopping centres, shopping at the more appealing supermarkets, and allowing days to unfold in these interior worlds where time passes with the electronic action of tills, the geography of retail architects, the smells of clothing, treated floors, cappuccino and food halls, the sounds of conversation, silver-toned spruikers with hand-held mikes and door-step speaker systems, children and the clacking of shoes, and Rose and I finding some measure of enjoyment in each other and the element of opportunity or surprise: there is always something we can do next. Otherwise I will go mad.

But it confounds my confidence in my own study. I've put so much work into this course. It *should* work at this, the most basic of all economic levels. Anyway, enough. Robert has said we should get together again. I would like that. I have missed male company for many a year, and he seems like a nice male.

*

Transport 2

There is something alienating about sliding into the driving seat of a car after years of travelling about in taxis and buses. Especially a big car, like the station wagon King's Company has purchased for us. Its moulded body and power-steering lend it an unreal feeling. Within weeks I have dented the front off-side fender by reversing out from the underground car-park that services King's Company's offices in the Cultural Centre. Motivating the moulded metal with the finger touch steering wheel and feather-light accelerator, it is easy to miss seeing the concrete pillar even if it is right beside me, especially if I am looking over my left shoulder to reverse out and keeping an eye on Rose at the same time, and trying to remember whether or not I put the timer on for the tuna pie. There are so many of them around, those concrete pillars. It's like a catacombs. But the sound of moulded fender collapsing in on itself against immutably squared concrete has a muted brutality.

Not that either Mei-ling or I care particularly. It is not really 'our' car. But it will be embarrassing for Mei-ling. And perhaps my carelessness disturbs her. Like my alcohol consumption, it makes her uncertain of Rose's safety in my hands. She has already said as much. We have had a nice, intimate Christmas. I feel we are together. But I am still carrying anger. I don't know why, but I am 'throwing my weight around' as we prepare to drive Mei-ling to work. Yes, come along Rose, forget that, we have to go. Mummy has to get to work. Are you ready Mei-ling? Anger flies from my back in hot drips as I move. It knocks invisible cups out of the way and tosses sheaves of air aside as it passes. Space might as well be an ensemble of rugby players tumbled out of the way as they try to wrestle me to the ground.

What am I angry about? Who knows: the budget that won't balance, having to get up and get Rose ready to drive Mei-ling to work when we'd both rather be doing something else, having to take Rose down to hang the washing out, not having enough time to myself, having a major MBA thesis to write and no time to get to the university to search the library for vital references, no time to myself, watching the consultancy skills I developed in Singapore, the business contacts, the prescience of what it takes to change the culture of an organisation through quality improvement techniques, the beginnings of a career, all gone on hold, a sense of loss of self as I immerse myself in Rose and yet I WANTED this, but no time to myself, getting around to the washing up only as I start to cook the evening meal so that if I don't get this done before we go to pick up Mei-ling it is still there sitting on the side when she walks in and that means I am not doing my job well enough even though Mei-ling and I have never talked about what that job is I've just taken it upon myself, no time for myself. Easier to drink wine once the sun goes down than use the considerable intrapersonal and interpersonal skills I have to address any of this no time to myself.

Phillipa coming back for a meal after work now. Good to see her. Nice to feel involved in conversations about the company. Feel I might have something to offer. But it's all King's Company. I am basically just the cook. Cook with attitude. But not feeling sorry for myself, no. Just angry. Angry and drinking wine while I cook. Relaxing into the cooking and drinking and listening. Hoping I have something to offer. But essentially an outsider. A non-worker now. A not-in-the-workforce person. A non-career-path-oriented person. Can't even find the time to work on the next degree because I use the time Rose is asleep to get down to hang the washing out and do all of those things that bore her. Again, not doing what I promised myself and making time for myself. Stupid, foolish man, not looking after himself and not caring for himself and not talking to anybody else about that. If you don't like it, get out. Too late for that. Just bottling it up and exuding the anger like an explosion of perspiration in slow motion.

And Mei-ling asks me what's wrong. And I say 'nothing' irritably. 'Look, it's fine' I say, sounding like it isn't. So we drive in silence. She tells me that sometimes she gets frightened. She doesn't know what is happening in the house with Rose when I am like this. I tell her I am fine. I don't hurt Rose. I wouldn't dream of hurting Rose. If I get angry with Rose I walk away for a while. I deal with myself. I don't drink until after six o-clock. Rose will be in bed soon. I am not irresponsible – although I do not say this. It is too humiliating to think that I am irresponsible and unable to adequately perform this role I have voluntarily taken on. I am a grown up. I am a mature adult. I can handle children. Especially my own daughter. This is fine. We play together. We find things to do.

But after I have dropped Mei-ling off, and left her with another serve of friable, stony silences to carry off with her for the day, I am driving back to our house to finish getting Rose dressed. I am driving through stupid bloody traffic, people in moulded cars jockeying for position on multi-lanes as if their lives depend upon it – winning and beating the next driver rather than simply getting there safely and in one piece. And this bus driver pulls out from the side into me. He has not even indicated until I am right beside him and he is literally pulling out into my vehicle, invading the ambient space of my (dented) moulded bodywork, before I even have time to check mirrors and see if I have time to change lanes. This driver has people onboard his bus and he is simply bullying me on the basis that he has right of way and he has more people on board than I do. There is no courtesy here. There is disregard for my safety, and the safety of my daughter, who is in the back. I have to brake suddenly, sounding my horn furiously at this driver. I spur my car around behind the bus, come up beside him on the inside lane, sounding my horn. Luckily there are traffic lights on the brow of the hill which turn red. He stops the bus. I get out of my car, leaving the engine running, and pound on the door of this bus. I pound and pound, shouting at the driver inside "What the fuck do you think you're doing? You don't just pull out into other traffic like that! What do you think you're doing?"

The driver tries to pretend I am not there. He has the safety of the bus's concertina doors, which do not give way even though I push at them and pound. The people on the bus are looking at me, but I

38

am not seeing them. I don't care. As the bus pulls off I get back into my car and slam the door shut and pull away, trying to take care to watch mirrors and do it all right, this strange and alien business of manoeuvring moulded metal forms on wheels in and out of straight lines and at right angles and curves. And in the back, my daughter says to me, "You're scaring me daddy."

And suddenly, at the wheel, still driving and checking mirrors, I find myself engulfed by giant mountains of sobs that wrack my body as if I were rupturing, granite shards falling away from my frame, landslides slipping from my back, the hot earth bubbling and churning in my belly.

I am not very good at this.

*

Parklands

I am calming down a bit. I think the tension is the role reversal stuff. Bit of a culture shock, perhaps. Rose and I have started to search out the 'green bits' on the map, and this is better. A bit of an adventure. Now that we have a car, we have an immediate freedom. When we first moved to Witherford Street, we were restricted to two – both just a block away. There is a vast difference, however, between pushing Rose around the block to the East King park –and all of the attendant preparations involved in that operation – and being able to jump into the car and zoom off across town to a distant green bit on the map. We are like explorers, threading our way through the criss-crossing squares and rectangles of urban planning, matching road names and landmarks nominated in the pale, two-dimensional colours of the street directory with the ungainly, fast-moving, three-dimensional relief of streetscape.

Our quest for parkland takes us into unchartered territory. The eastern and northern districts of King open up to us, become known as a network of grass sanctuaries, much as the land out west is known to pilots by its sun-dipped coins of pastoral dam.

With the car, I don't have to bother with the pusher. We park the car beside the playground, and then get into it to go home. Or we are at the shop for a drink or something to eat in an instant.

As a male primary care giver, I guess I had expected to be different. That the role would demand other qualities of me. Instead I find I am geared towards the achievable and achievement far more than the process of getting there. My focus is on the product, the end result. The 'playing'. The 'buying'. The 'eating' or 'drinking'.

And yet the car does provide me with a process, and one I can enjoy with Rose. We sing on the way, for instance. I can smile at her in the rear-view mirror – which I twist as we drive so that she can see I am talking to her. In the pusher, I am always above and behind her. The world is always in front. When I point at things, I have to drop my hand to her eye level and extend it unnaturally in front, so that she can follow it. In the pusher Rose may be in my 'pouch', but it is a pouch separated by the tubular technology of metal frame and wheels.

And then there is the radio and CD player for those longer journeys – again, CDs of songs she hears on the tv, plus others I am in a position to screen for her, as I edit out what I think of as dross and received culture from Rose's early life. Should I have this power? I have it anyway. Best to wield it well. No crummy Disney tunes – she will pick those up soon enough. No commercial tv. Again, she will access that as soon as she learns her way around a remote control. No shopping malls with cheap performance acts designed to sell products. Rose and I, as much as possible, now do parks.

In the park, Rose is learning all the time. Each time she practices a new skill, takes a new risk. I always encourage her, but at her own pace. I also emphasise her own sense of "feeling safe". "Yes, try that. Does it feel safe?" I fear she must, however, be able to read the "no"s in my body language. Even though I was a personal risk taker when I was a kid, I am a very nervous Dad. I am always following her through the climbing frame and slide combo with my hand extended towards the space she occupies. And I am always there, reaching for and withdrawing from her, as she tries to balance her way along a low, snaking beam.

As Rose gains skill and confidence, I relax. I started taking a book, and will sit nearby and read while Rose plays. Parks become for me a rare opportunity to extend my mind into the oxygen-rich warmth of these generous arbours of open space. Such a relief after the cramped confines of Singapore. I stretch out mentally, take in the sun intellectually, let the air get to my brain. I begin the literature search for my thesis in Rose's "nap times" at home, which brings the uni books in the post, and these in turn accompany us to the park. And so knowledge becomes a product of the park for both Rose and myself, each in our respective ways.

But it is not just for the two of us. There are always those chance meetings – another parent with a child. Rose spots them before I do. Watches them cautiously for a while, but then swiftly makes her way towards them. Looks into their eyes – something about a pair of eyes at her level. Action precedes words. She gets on the piece of play equipment they are on. Or they get on hers. Or the two go to a new piece of play equipment together, and start to play.

As parents we love aiding them in this – putting them on either end of a see-saw, or on a roundabout together. I am never sure whether this is because we see the benefit for the child or because we simply want to have a natter with another parent. For me it is never the latter, because I find talking to strangers uncomfortable, an effort I hate. I am thus a minimalist in such situations, talking about the weather, talking about the park, talking about Rose and the way the children are getting on, and leaving it at that. The immediate context. If I were a woman I would be more conversational. And most of the other parents I meet are women – although I am surprised by the increasing number of men these days. But I find it easy with neither gender. And the kids play with each other regardless.

And lastly, there is that feature of parks that enables Rose to do something she was never easily able to do in Singapore, and could not do so easily when the impetus of our journeys was moderated by the pusher: run. It is to do with being able to get there quickly, get on with the climbing and sliding and swinging upon release from the car, and carry that same energy forward out across the full extent of green landscape available to her. Rose runs. She will get off one piece of equipment and just go for it – out into the centre of the park (never, thankfully, towards a road). And I will run after her. And after a bit of running, she will turn and look back from where she has come. As if she is estimating how far she has travelled. Computing the change in perspective around her. As if her ability to do this gives her yet another capacity for achievement. Another dimension to space. Rose and I, running through the parklands. Laughing and calling. But never chasing. I don't want it to be a chase.

*

Lounge

Mei-ling's end-of-the-working-day is becoming another feature in the relief of Rose's and my day that is has been enabled by the car. There is always an element of uncertainty about it, because Mei-ling rings when she is ready to come home. Sometimes that is closer to seven o'clock than six. So there is always a sense of the workplace holding home to ransom. This is a minor impingement; one I am generally able to arrange my preparations for the evening around.

I feed Rose in the lounge around five anyway, and prepare an evening meal at the same time. I usually leave the washing up from the night before until then, so that I can include in it the pots, pans and utensils used to prepare the evening meal. So that when Mei-ling comes home, the washing up will be done, the kitchen benches clean, and a meal on the go.

When the phone call comes, I gather Rose up from the lounge (where I can watch her from the kitchen) and we descend to the car. So much of our daily life at home revolves around the lounge. It's where Rose's play things cascade out from her bedroom, and from which they are re-assembled back into their rightful places in her bedroom before dinner. It's where she watches t.v. or listens to music while I make preparations in the kitchen, either before breakfast, before taking Mei-ling to work, or for lunch, or for dinner. And it's the space we leave in order to pick up Mei-ling.

Rose is usually looking forward to seeing Mummy. And Mummy is invariably looking forward to seeing Rose. And I am generally glad to facilitate this daily reunion, as well as being anxious to get Mei-ling away from what to me is the source of tension, imposition and debilitation in her life – this large, unwieldy, unheeding, unlearning and inefficient company which Mei-ling devotes herself to ferrying through the awkward and uncertain waters of cultural as well as structural organisation change.

I admire Mei-ling for doing this, and want very much to help her. Organisational change isn't Mei-ling's area of expertise. She is primarily a creative director who knows a lot about running cultural tourism organisations and crafting from them a certain functionality that stands outside the patriarchal square. I don't necessarily have the skills to achieve what I have seen Mei-ling achieve in past companies she has run – in fact, I know I couldn't do this myself. But I can provide Mei-ling with the theoretical underpinnings for what she is trying to achieve.

And I always do this at home, in private, as we debrief her day over a meal - again in our lounge. We have always eaten in the lounge. Never had a dining room, or a dining table. And over the years in Singapore, with Bahasa Huaya Tamil, it was over dinner in the lounge that I developed the habit of facilitating Mei-ling's reflections on her work. The processing of her day.

I realised after a while that there is a great deal of power for me in cultivating this role for myself in my loved one's life. It actually gives me a place in her work denied to most other housewives, because I am not forever committed to asking open questions designed to solicit conversation and then offer supportive comment. I actually have knowledge and expertise to contribute, and can track the impact of my input over time.

Sometimes Phillipa comes back, and shares our meal. And the evening, and our lounge, is full of three-way analysis of the company and its potentials, current barriers and explanations for these, strategies for overcoming them. So Mei-ling's work titrates into the home environment, as it did in Singapore. But the conduit through which the human embodiments of this titration move from one vessel to another – from workplace to home – is devoid to the pressures of the workplace itself. When Rose and I enter Mei-ling's workplace, it is the workplace that changes.

It's like we bring our lounge with us, and unleash it on the unwitting geography of the protestant work ethic. Rose always runs on ahead to find Mummy, and those office staff remaining at that time of day accommodate her gladly. They are pretty much all women, some with kids of their own, some not. But they all enjoy the arrival of this young willy willy of childhood in their workspace. And, although they do not bring their own children and grandchildren to work, it adds a strong modelling dimension in the workplace, that the boss's 2 year-old daughter comes to pick her up. Even if Mei-ling is in a meeting, Rose still bounds in and is incorporated into the process –if only for the moment it takes Mei-ling to welcome her, and arrange for her either to return to me or go off with another member of staff.

I think I also have part in this process as a man. They all know, for instance, that I look after Rose during the day, so I am something of an oddity – a soft male rather than a member of the 'ruling class'. Nevertheless, I exert masculine pressures. I use my silence a lot – make small talk where appropriate, offer supportive comment to members of staff on work they either talk to me about or of which I know through Mei-ling. But on the whole, I urge my purpose on the workplace through that very masculine combination of presence and taciturnity. I am here for one thing – to take Mei-ling away from all this – and I will not go away until she comes with me. It is a cogent imperative to exert, and I am uncertain of its morality, but desire its result for 'us', not just for me. That's my excuse anyway.

So for Mei-ling, Rose brings a little of the joy from home into her workplace at the end of the day, and I bring the pull of home, the unspoken pressure to come back to it, to detach herself from the bond of the workplace. I bring a masculine construction of home into the workplace, while Rose acts as a catalyst to free the workplace from patriarchal constraints Mei-ling doesn't want in it anyway. And between the three of us, we facilitate this complex process of extraction from work to home such that Mei-ling's homecomings never ape that factitious separation between the two encapsulated in "Daddy's home!" I know Rose is too young to understand this, but I hope so much it is something she 'learns' in time. Though I still worry that as a man I'm not suited to this role. The primary carer.

POTENTIAL RESEARCH TOPIC: Home~work intersubjectivity – effects on productivity? Workplace satisfaction ~ productivity. Do the profits go up or down?

*

Windows

Robert Cunningham visited yesterday. We sat on the front veranda while Rose played and had a nice, non-masculine males' chat. It is strange forming relationships with men again, especially men of my own cultural background. I never really formed friendships with any in Singapore. Mei-ling has offered him a position with the company – she needs a business development manager. He says he's not sure it's the sort of opportunity he is looking for with the company at this time. He had viewed the move to King as a window of opportunity, but now he's here it's a window he doesn't want to force open. Business training on the job has schooled him to motivate himself and address task, analyse and review and form objectives and plan strategically, with specific business targets and goals you work towards on a daily basis. Keep a record of progress, opportunities created, openings engineered, deals closed, stakeholders networked.

I'm familiar with all of this, but more from a theoretical perspective. Robert has picked his knowledge up along the way, as he's needed it. But he is looking now for an alternative to the objectifying nature of traditional business. Even when businessmen express emotion, he said, it is designed to create an effect beyond the emotion itself. It is networking, or relationship-building, or sealing the deal, or using empathy to identify the needs of the customer. The affective aspect of human being is purely functional. The patriarchal world of business is not human. Humans are just instrumental in it.

He says that business is not necessarily anathema to the community development ethics of cultural tourism, nor to the sort of sensibilities he experiences in his relationships with people as a gay man. But believes the discourse of business is in need of transformation. And his way of doing that at the moment, he has decided, is to remove the element of 'forcing' from the process. He wants to see what happens, not what he makes happen. He wants to look beyond the window, for the other party in the opportunity to make the offer, to help him lift the sash and step through.

I identified with this notion of surrendering control over the dominant paradigm. Early in our relationship Mei-ling went me relentlessly over my desire to control in this way.

I had always thought myself well-versed in feminist ideology, but I was astounded – and highly confronted – to be faced with the inveterate nature of my socialisation as a man. It wasn't just opening doors for ladies and dominating the discussion – it came right down to the very way I used language itself: the use of questions, for instance, to retain control of the conversation. The reduction of content to my sense of logic, the insistence on words as the primary medium of expression. I found myself watching my every word (to my anger and frustration), and she was right: I used them to force any interpretation of a discussion towards my construction of it. Language was a medium of control, and I had to re-learn how to use it.

I never have, of course. But at least I can understand something of Robert's quest for an 'alternative' to the dominant business paradigm. I like the idea of redefining the window and what motivates its instrumentality as 'opportunity'. In a sense, I have seized a similar window in taking on the role of primary care-giver with Rose. It's the best chance I can imagine to become something useful in this world; to restructure my socialisation. To look for what will happen next rather than force it. And with Rose, plenty happens next.

But I have also placed a cap on the experience – a limit to its duration. After that, I will have a qualification that will, I hope, take me into sinecure, a university post somewhere. Or I could take on the challenge of re-entering the private sector, armed with my self-transformation and my new Masters – both forms of new knowledge – and invest in the project of change from within.

And I wonder if I can do that, too. Without 'forcing the sash'. Whether I actually have the courage. I remember the vertigo I experienced in Singapore, as we went from one high-rise apartment to another looking for somewhere to rent, and I found myself retreating more and more towards the centre of the room. It wasn't until then that I realised I had the condition. So we had to sacrifice the much-prized view for a low-rise apartment in a not-so-new quarter – a decision none of our Singaporean colleagues could understand.

Fear is a bodily reaction that surprises us. So much so that we institutionalise to contain it. When Mei-ling moved her company offices in Singapore, they had to get a geomancer in to check out the *feng shui* of the new premises. Mei-ling was forced to have a lace-curtain hung across her window because a palm tree outside represented bad *feng shui* – literally, its blade-like fronds stabbing her in the back. In Western culture we would call it superstition, but in Chinese culture *feng shui* institutionalises fear such that it retains a credible cultural instrumentality.

Robert glanced across at the huge palm tree that stood in out front garden, not metres from the glass that separates it from our bedroom. He asked if we had a lace curtain here too. I admitted that we do, but only because we like lace curtains.

Evidently Dale likes to sleep without curtains and with the window open. I wondered whether this was a cultural thing, because Dale is of Aboriginal descent, but Robert seemed to think he just liked the fresh air. It infuriates Robert because he can't sleep once daylight breaks. So he sleeps with his back to the window, to maximise his own shadow. And since Dale sleeps facing the window, to make the most of the fresh air, this means that they either sleep back to back or face to face. I like the idea of face-to-face better. Exchanging breath as they sleep, like Maoris in greeting. Window as witness.

*

Entertainment Area

I always feel awkward being "dressed up". Mei-ling used to do it in Singapore too. We would just be window-shopping, a pastime so many other Singaporeans enjoyed on their weekends, and I'd be looking at a really nice coat or a jacket, and Mei-ling would want to buy it for me. Well, I don't really need it, I would say. But she would persist. "Why no-o-o-o-ot?" she would ask, sending up her own Chineseness. In the end, I would give in. I always loved the item of clothing, and would wear it forever. But there is something deep within my own upbringing that says: you don't spend that sort of money on yourself.

At least here it is truly functional. I need a good outfit to attend the opening night of a promotion. One of my "duties" as partner to the Creative Director and CEO of the state's tourism commission. But the cheque is more than a week's salary for Mei-ling. The brogues feel great, but. Like I am walking on expensive wood. And when we attend the opening night of the first cultural promotion of Mei-ling's first year with King's Company, I feel very well-presented.

I am not good on these occasions. I want to support Mei-ling very much. I try to stick by her as much as possible, so that I can lift the conversation from her from time to time, give her the opportunity to relax and mentally regroup so that she can initiate instead of responding. She doesn't really know any of these people but they all know each other, and each other's agendas.

So one of her Commissioners, Jane Barrimore, wants her to meet the Pro-Vice-Chancellor from her uni because she's a lecturer and the Pro-Vice is keen on recruiting international students, and Mei-ling has Southeast Asian connections. And because Jane's husband, Derek Barrimore, is Chair of the Commission, Mei-ling particularly has to oblige. Then Derek himself wants Mei-Ling to meet some Board members from Doherty's, the grain exporters, because he thinks there is potential in the South-east Asian market for northern Australian grain.

The Tourism Department's own nominee on the Commission, Harold Winterbourne then takes her across to the Minister for Tourism and the Arts because Mei-ling needs to start persuading the Minister that Max Kingsbury's proposal for the company's "home", the Next Stage, is unacceptable; it reduces the company to the temporary status of a tenant, rather than resident. Mei-ling's proposal can only work if King's Company is taking the lead, performing arts activity slotting in around her tourism activity, so that she can forge professional relations with the artists themselves and co-opt them into her tourism activity. At an event like this, the networking pressures just domino.

Despite my negative disposition to it, I can be quite good at personalising a conversation, or using my ignorance as an outsider and non-tourism-person to ask an intelligent question. But what's happening at King's Company functions is that I am being sidelined. Mei-ling is whisked away by one agenda after another and I am left with the partners of minor players. In other words, as a partner, I find myself talking to young travel consultants or middle-aged ticketing agents while Mei-ling is escorted away by Phillipa or the Chair to a you-must-meet-so-and-so. And I find myself engaging in polite talk standing on the edge of a milieu, watching people in formal attire who are also standing around ("circulating"), all holding champagne glasses like myself, between finger and thumb by the base rather than the stem, watching Mei-ling at a distance.

Robert Cunningham isn't sidelined in the same way. I guess because he's on the Tourism Australia Council. But he's always there beside Dale, and Dale always introduces him, and involves him in the conversation with whomever Dale is networking with. At one point it is Mei-ling, because Mei-ling wants to interest Dale in committing Cult Tourism to a joint community development / cultural tourism project with her, working with the lower-paid ethnic minorities and, of course, the local indigenous population. I don't mean to be rude but Dale doesn't come across as massively 'indigenous' to me, but he seems happy to get onto the bandwagon. And certainly talks the talk well.

I love watching Mei-ling at work. She is a tremendously respectful person. She puts up with all sorts of interpersonal rubbish I know I would find it difficult to tolerate. People at this level in a society – the lawyers and doctors and business executives and parliamentarians and senior bureaucrats – are invariably circumspect, but they rarely lose an opportunity to patronise or deliver barely veiled criticism. And Mei-ling's intelligence always works overtime, hearing the loading, identifying the obvious and sought-for reaction, checking it, identifying her own agenda, and formulating a response which moves the issue forward rather than engages in unnecessary and unconstructive competitive conflict.

She does all of this whilst holding a steady gaze, an equanimity of poise, composure of face. I am sure people don't notice the thoughts even crossing her mind, and are disarmed by the response. Only I know what is happening in her head, after years of standing beside her while she does it and then debriefing with her afterwards.

Even from a distance I can follow what is happening in Mei-ling's mind by watching her eyes. I love Mei-ling's eyes. Her face has an almost aristocratic asian-ness. Even though she is Chinese in ethnicity, the fineness of her features looks Siamese or something more associated in those oriental mythologies of the nineteenth century with monarchy and royalty. But there is an imperceptibility about the line where her eyelid meets with her beautiful, doe-brown eye that gives away her thoughts and feelings. I marvel at the subtlety of it.

*

Wainscotting

Arte de Leon has done a bunk. In the same week as the first promotion in Mei-ling's program, with some immediate critical acclaim in the travel press, the man who failed to get her job tries to steal the limelight. It couldn't be more orchestrated. His name is down on the program as the 'star' of a major Pacific Rim promotion mid-year with Ranald Whippett from the National Tourism Commission, and as the main presenter in Mei-ling's debut at the end of the year, a South East Asia extravaganza based on Shakespeare's *A Midsummer Night's Dream*. And now he flies out in a flurry of press, saying there is not enough work to keep him here. He just *has* to go overseas *(darling)*(the man behaves more like a ham actor than a credible luminary in the tourism industry).

Apparently he often does this – runs back to England for a bit to top up his I'm-an-experienced-tour-director credentials in the old colonialists' cultural Mecca. Then comes back with fistfulls of itineraries and pamphlets and press, and numerous additions to his cv, all of which he brandishes but never actually releases to anyone in case they discover just how paltry his role actually was. Talks loudly instead at promotions and launches and in private soirees about this famous cruise director or that famous tour operator and when-I-was-in-Athens-with-the-National-Line-(UK-of-course).

A couple of fans who remember the days of the cruise had letters in the local daily the day after his departure, lamenting his loss. Of course Phillipa is yet to finalise the contracting, thinking she had months yet. So Mei-ling will look foolish in front of her Commission, even though they must be as wise to de Leon as Mei-ling now is, since they didn't give him the job.

I wrote a poem once which began with the lines:

You have emerged from my conception

Like a slug from the wainscotting

It was a vituperative piece about a former girlfriend, but it seems particularly appropriate for de Leon. Wainscottings are such an artifice - cover up the gaping lateral shaft of air between the wall and the floor, and the mess the carpenter, bricklayer or plasterer made at the edges of their work. They disguise lashings of sloppy and illegal electric wiring, and, yes, slugs.

In Cooksland the slugs come out when you are not looking and slither across the carpet to some secret feast you never uncover, and certainly aren't invited to. You only know they have been because they leave a slithery, slimy trail which is dry by the time you get up, and has been fingered by Rose and brought to her mouth before you have the presence of mind to say "Stop!", or reach her to prevent the hand from delivering the foul residue to an innocent mouth.

*

Recreation

It's so great to be back in a country where outdoor performance has become the norm. Not that it was uncommon in Singapore. There was Hindu New Year and Chinese New Year and Dragon Boat Races and the Autumn Lantern Festival and a whole host of ancestor worship celebrations. Almost any excuse, it seemed, and I loved it. Community celebrations grounded in mythology which link 'the people' to the seasons and nature and time of year, as well as providing periodic relief from the routine of 'toil'.

Whereas in Australia, all we have is a handful of Christian vestiges and horse racing or bank holidays even the banks don't seem to get these days. So we've had to create festivals, to celebrate our ethnic minorities, to celebrate our industries (the wine and music festivals, agricultural, industry showcases at the capital city convention centres). Mei-ling says there is a deeper cultural heritage that than. Aboriginal storytelling performances were always out-of-doors. And never set in concrete – changed as the stories and the circumstances in which they occurred changed. Characters in much Aboriginal mythology were like next-door neighbours. Spoken about as if known intimately. As if there beside you – even though for the most part they existed in this entire other world that was supposed to have created the world. A homely but vibrant tradition which embraced the plurality of time and person.

I think our contemporary Australian outdoor celebrations owe more to the community arts movements of the 1970s and 80s than anything else. It was this that provided the springboard for the cultural tourism movement. It's comforting to return after a period away and find a degree of ease and professionalism in the execution of them these days. Especially to experience it vicariously through Rose's senses, because of course it is all new to her. This is the cultural landscape her mother's company will occupy in the coming years.

We wheel the pusher round a bend in the path, between two huge Moreton Bay Fig trees, and there are a group of street musicians coming towards us playing a variety of brass and stringed instruments, each with a different outsized hat shaped like a piece of giant fruit. We can slip between two rocks towards the purpose-built 'natural' pool and there will be three acrobats blending their work into the rockface. Down near the kiosk there are a troupe of ethnic dancers – Lithuanian, I think – clearly a community group who have given up their own time this fine

Wednesday afternoon – who are teaching some dances to anyone who wants to join in. Rose has no hesitation in joining in.

In the open-air amphitheatre is a contemporary dance troupe who have developed a piece about the animals of the continents – they stretch, contort, leap and glide, emulating the form and movement of one animal after another, eliding oceans with musical bridges that sound like an original score. Then there is a larger, covered amphitheatre in which a unique troupe of youth acrobats called the Balancing Bananas perform a full, two hour circus-tent routine of immense skills and imagination. There is a multi-school spectacular in which local high schools have each contributed their version of the Year of Human Rights, brought together by a team of professional artists who have helped the teenagers develop their own performances which, nevertheless, fit into a whole. It's a promenade event that takes over the whole Parkland for an afternoon. Everywhere you go, led by a team of storytellers, something springs out at you, kids rush in, rush out, something magic emerges from a bower.

And from the very large to the very small, even at the exit to the Parklands a group of kids from a local school have got together and are busking with flutes and violins. Rose and I stop to listen. She is entranced. Then there is face-painting and puppet-making there, giant puppets here, and marionettes in the Little Theatre at the Performance Centre. It is a magical fortnight. And a chance for Rose to see that what we do at home happens elsewhere – that other kids do it. Part of reality.

It also gives me a break from having to be the endless source of voices and antics for Rose's glove puppets. I made the mistake of doing it to entertain her. Another masculine trait I find within myself – to perform and do it *for* Rose, as opposed to facilitating Rose's process of play. Try as I might, I find myself ineluctably falling into the commedia-punchinello knockabout routines I grew up with as a kid. I want so much to be 'other', to be different, and find ways outside the patriarchal norm. But what comes 'naturally' has an inherent timbre of violence running through it.

And Rose loves it – to the point of distraction. "Talk him","Talk her". So the Festival of Youth is a holiday for me too – because everybody else is "talking" – talking their characters, talking their bodies, talking their instruments, talking paint on paper, talking shapes against the rocks. It's everywhere. I just have to relax and enthuse and push the pusher because it is too much to expect Rose to walk the entire Parklands all day long.

An opportunity too for Rose to actually see something produced by her mother. She was too young in Singapore. Now she is alert and excited and understands that this is what mummy 'does'. And although Mei-ling has made a conscious choice to hold over her own official promotional 'debut' with King's Company until the end of the year, she could not resist doing an infant's promotion for the Festival of Youth. I think secretly this is the stuff Mei-ling likes the best – the educational interface of cultural tourism, with little kids, where it really amazes and engages. But it also gives her the opportunity to model in microcosm the strategy she will use to firstly introduce cultural tourism promotions into the performing arts agenda, and then co-opt the latter into the former.

It is a charming piece developed by a friend of Phillipa's, Jennifer Fellowes, back-to-backing neatly with a number of more traditional theatre-style productions on in the Little Theatre during the Festival. Mei-ling persuaded Dale Balanda and another new graduate to involve some of Cult Tourism's clientele in the event, and Rose got to meet the talent afterwards, as well the musician who accompanies the show live. It is a wonderful experience for all of us. So sad that Max Kingsbury has to utilise even something as pure and simple as this as an opportunity to engage in a little institutional colonisation of King's Company.

He is well aware that for Mei-ling this is an opportunity to demonstrate how the relationship between King's Company and the King performing arts community will eventually work. In the future, it is King's Company that will be running and marketing the Festival of Youth as a cultural tourism event, in which a promotional event by King's Company will be a central feature. He recognises this is a chance for Mei-ling to 'put her toe in the water'. So he's out for a spoiler from the beginning.

First he complains that he was not shown the 'script', which of course he wasn't, because there is no script in the sense he understands. There is a project plan and a scenario. Then he objects to the fact that he was not invited to the 'dress rehearsals', even though they are not 'dress rehearsals' in the theatrical tradition. And finally – and, it's tempting to suggest, as a result – he refuses to acknowledge the promotion in newspaper advertising as a Kings Company event. All 'productions' in the Festival are 'a Performance Centre production', he argues – for ease of marketing and 'brand identification'. Whereas in reality most of the other major participants get a "The Performance Centre presents…" or "Festival of Youth presents…" The difficulty, he says, is in categorising 'this sort of performance'.

Robert said even the most incompetent analyst would be hard pressed not to see that Kingsbury is clearly working the "new girl" over. The games these boys play, we laughed. Nevertheless, the event is a success for Mei-ling. Although it doesn't get any press, word of mouth seems to build audiences.

NOTE: Connell's notion of culture as 'practice'; what we do, like an artisan or tradesperson; as distinct from the usual 'values, beliefs, ceremonies' notion of culture, and the behavioural manifestation of this in most organisational culture theory. 'practice' is not the same as 'behaviour'. 'practice is learned, and passed on, and contains norms and embedded ideas and beliefs.

'practice' is what Kingsbury is engaging in – ways he has learnt of wielding power, The patriarchal ideology is buried deep within. It 'operates' his tactics, almost without him being aware of it. But this is too anthropomorphic or teleological. Ideology cannot have a volitionality of its own. It isn't 'power'. It doesn't even have its own consciousness.

*

Door Jamb

I seem to have spent so much of my life leaning against the door jamb. I remember as a youth at parties, it was my preferred spot – neither in one room nor the other, but able to observe what was going on in both and dip into the passing trade. Nothing permanent. Nothing you had to commit to. Just conversations against the general barrage of background noise. Fragments of words and vowels, head and face language augmented by hands and body twists, banking up the room into a muted buffer of communication. And outside it was cold and dark, your breath clouded in the night air and footsteps fell brittle against the chill quartz-halogen streetlamps. Cars passed with steely insouciance.

That was in the UK, of course. But even here in King, in our weatherboard house in warmth of northern Australia, I lean in the door jamb to listen to Phillipa and Mei-ling work their way through the political intricacies of King's Company and the Cooksland tourism scene, and how it can link in with the performing arts in a way that enhances the profitability of the latter, as per Mei-ling's brief. I make my own contributions as best I can, because basically I am preparing tea in the kitchen.

Last night I spent a full evening sitting with my back square against the jamb of the front door, while Phillipa sat against the front porch verandah doors (which I only finished painting recently – months after we had them installed). She had come back from Sydney early, leaving Mei-ling to pow-wow with the Creative Directors of the Big Six. The general managers only stay for the first couple of days, it seems. They do their talking behind closed doors, on interstate visits. I ask her if this doesn't create a second layer of managerial leadership which might undermine the superstructure represented by the executive.

This is something we have talked about before, and I know she and Mei-ling have agreed that they want an open management which works outside the traditional patriarchal paradigm. Since we've been in Singapore, all of the state tourism commissions have adopted the Surrey Street model of a joint leadership of Creative Director and General Manager. It is actually Mei-ling who is breaking ground by re-introducing the role of the CEO, and combining it with the creative role. Mei-ling and Phillipa have employed a marketing executive – a first for King's Company – and promoted Juneen from a general administrator role to the executive level as production manager, so that they have a management executive rather than a hierarchy with a Creative Director and General Manager duopoly over a layer of middle management.

It has been my advice that they adopt this 'flat structure'. I also introduced Mei-ling to the version of situational leadership she is adopting, working in consultation with all staff to a level dependent on individual competence and performance. This is very different from the model pushed by the government bureaucracies for so long – of the creative director isolated in their own office, in which they are supposed to sit and "create", while the general manager really runs the show through a stable of administrators and production staff.

But I have concerns about the internal consistency of the King's Company model in implementation: on one hand they want an element of consensus to pervade their decision-making, to make decisions without hierarchies, but on the other hand both Mei-ling and Phillipa make unilateral decisions in the course of a day's work that affect not only each other and the rest of the management team but, more importantly, the rest of the staff. The action of decision works counter to what they are trying to achieve.

I am not saying it can't work. I very much want it to work. There is nothing I am reading currently which convinces me that traditional organisational culture is succeeding to effect change anywhere in the world that takes it beyond the patriarchal construction of "competition" as "natural", the basis for economy. In a humane world, we desperately need an alternative.

But I am concerned for Mei-ling and Phillipa, I suppose. They are under scrutiny – all of the local travel businesses, as well as the various government funding and auspicing bodies, both here and interstate, are watching the King's Company management "experiment". For it to either succeed or, I am sure for the men involved, to fail. So expectations are high and Mei-ling and Phillipa can't afford the luxury of failure. And, as Phillipa points out, I have a Masters thesis at stake here!

As we talk, I watch Phillipa's features disappear gradually into the fading light. We are not officially into winter, and yet these mildly sub-tropical evenings linger and the soft, golden light reddens slowly and slips away to pale embers against the occasional drifts of cloud. I'm aware it is a long time since I have had a conversation with her by myself, and she comments on the fact. Says I am as intellectual as ever.

I never see myself as an intellectual, but know I dwell disproportionately in the cognitive part of my brain, at the expense of other more feeling sentience where intelligence might also lie. Phillipa, on the other hand, did her Masters in soft marketing, and the collocation of emotion and body image in the manufacture and selling of cosmetics. I can't imagine anybody with less of an interest in cosmetics. She never wears any. Has never needed to. If anything, there is just a little kohl around the eyes – which must be there for what reason?

I ask her, laughing, for her eyes are already rimmed with her own dark lashes and freckles. This is a woman who goes bushwalking alone up in the Kimberleys of North Western Australia and camps on the top of ancient rock formations beside three hundred metre waterfalls. She is stout but athletic in build, always seems to be in excellent health and is, frankly, stunningly beautiful. I find her dark brown eyes, thick-inlaid eyebrows and rich, purposeful lips almost too much to look at sometimes. I can't imagine kissing her. I certainly can't imagine being sexually intimate with her. Her body's workability and muscular thoroughness overwhelm me.

She tells me it is the nearest thing she has to a mask – just the sketch of one, but at least one she knows is there. I've never thought of her as someone who needs even a hint of a mask, and tell her so. I have known her since university. I know the men she has been in love with. She says she knows people always think of her as competent and beautiful and as someone who manages most things well. But inside there is someone who has never actually managed her self at all, and whom she has nurtured since she was a child.

She spoke of the loss of her mother – who died very early in her life, I know; she was brought up by her elder sisters and father (an all-female family of siblings). For this reason she has often wondered whether she is gay, but knows her desire for men and lust for sexual relations with them contradicts any such notion. Perhaps she is bi. She has tried relations with both sexes (I know this too) but the women always remain friends really, whereas the men she falls in love with, loses herself to for a while, and then repulses. She knows she does this, but can't work out why.

Perhaps, she says, it is because they cannot live up to the image she has of her father – the immeasurable love for him she has carried from her early years. He too died when she was young – around puberty. Which is the sort of coincidence psychologists have a field day with. Indeed, she has been in therapy for years, and things don't seem to improve for her. Then she asked me how I was getting on with Robert Cunningham, and whether I liked him. I thought the connection was curious and sudden, but didn't say so. I said we got on well. She said she had thought we would. That seemed to be all there was to the enquiry.

*

Education

I am learning a lot from Jennifer. I have started to pay her to babysit Rose from time to time, so that I can work on my thesis. It turns out she started out studying child care, before she turned to cultural tourism. She plays with Rose on Rose's level. But with equanimity, as in: she manages to speak and act like an adult. It's very clever. I forever notice myself, against all of my best intentions, descending into 'baby talk' with Rose. Now that she is so mobile and articulate herself, I am managing to claw my way back out of it again, but I still find myself notching up the pitch and using a patronisingly sing-song "Well what will we do now then?" rhetoric.

Somehow, sitting in the study concentrating on the highly intellectual pursuit of analysing a literature search places me in a very 'adult' place, from which it seems all too easy to see my own failing as primary care giver. Because it's not just that Jennifer herself is young and studying at uni. Mei-ling, when she has the time, has exactly the same ability to enter into 'play' with Rose that I lack. I find myself employing two key strategies: I create and monitor learning opportunities for Rose, and I 'perform' for her as her dad – do funny voices for the puppets etc.. But I don't enter into extended periods of actual play with her. I don't have the patience for it. I want to do other things with my mind.

I am sure this is a result of my socialisation as a man, but I don't know that I have the patience to change it. If I entered into it regularly, maybe I would settle into the practice. But I am still too driven by a sense of what it is *I* need to achieve, what *I* need to do. And yet I wanted this opportunity, to explore another side of myself, to form a relationship with Rose I know my father never had with me.

I talk to Jennifer about this, in dribs and drabs. Usually when I take a break from the study, and we have a coffee on the back or front veranda. Just as she 'plays' with Rose, she also enters into an 'adult' conversation with me very easily. And I with her.

I'm finding this 'forming relationships' thing refreshing, having not been able to do it in Singapore. First with Robert, and now with Jennifer. When Phillipa first introduced us, it was very much one of those "I must introduce you to so-and-so, you'll get along famously" set-ups. And I don't know if it's a peculiarly hunter-male thing but in those circumstances there is always an undercurrent anticipation of an impending "match". Even though I actually have no desire to enter into a one-on-one intimate relationship with anyone other than Mei-ling, let alone an affair, there is always a level of intelligence working somewhere down around the loins, as if my dick is independent of the rest of me and has this direct link to the centre of my mind that pops up (so to speak) from time to time with a sort-of limbic tugging at the sleeve: This one! Look at this one! She'll do. Can we stick it in, d'y'think?

So it was with Phillipa's 'matchmaking' on this occasion. And it was a relief to find when I finally met Jennifer that, while I like her easily, I don't find her sexually attractive. Which means we get to talk without an apparent gender-based agenda. She talks about her love life, and playing with kids, and King's performing arts scene, with which she has some cross-over. It's interesting to find out how distant they are from Mei-ling's and the state-government's strategy. Don't seem to understand it at all, which presents a significant communication challenge for Mei-ling.

Anyway, it's nice having friends again. In Singapore, it was only Mei-ling and me. Every other contact was work-related.

Not that my conversations with Jennifer are independent of work. Mei-ling is currently in a wrangle with the Cooksland Education Department over an interactive piece Jennifer has written for the company's young people's wing, Bower Bird. They have refused to allow it into schools until a range of scenes involving Aboriginal languages are removed, on the grounds that English is Australia's first language and Aboriginal language use is marginal compared to other Languages Other Than English. They said it was okay if a "balanced view" is put – but clearly what they mean by a balanced view is one that is explicated there and then in the performance elements of the piece, rather than in complementary educational notes.

This is clearly anti-indigenous ideological interference and Mei-ling won't have a bar of it. She simply pulled the promotion out of the Department's review process and sold it independently to any schools brave enough to take it. She has now refused to put any material before the Department's Review Board, which is causing great affront to the Education hierarchy. It has even reached the ears of the Minister for Education – such that the Minister for Arts and Tourism is muttering to senior King's Company Commission members about the state government's funding for the youth arm of the state's tourism commission.

Mei-ling is not overly perturbed. She knows that the only reason Bower Bird has continued this long is because the state government recognises it has to maintain some semblance of a cultural education program in schools. Since their emphasis on the 3Rs and IT has virtually driven any activity even remotely dealing with emotional intelligence out of the classroom, this token presence of 'performance' in schools is politically essential. And at least it's not 'theatre'!

Nevertheless, Jennifer is feeling a bit like the meat in the sandwich, and worried for her own future. As a cultural tourism specialist with earl childhood interests, it will not be easy to find work without a professional relationship with the state education system. Yet here she is clearly being marked out as an antagonist. She says she doesn't mind, because she is completely in favour ideologically. But I can hear that she is uncomfortable.

Anyway, in such a context it's kind of her to say that I am 'far from the worst of parents' she has come across. For most of them, she says, it's feed-em-and-clothe-em. Indeed, she seems almost impressed with my relationship with Rose, and that is heartening given that she does it so well.

*

Family Room

I have found a playgroup. Saw an advert at the local deli just around the corner. Just starting up, looking for interested parents. The inaugural meeting was at the local Anglican Church Hall. A lady from the Playgroup Association was setting it up. She had someone there from a recently formed playgroup in New King, on the north side, who talked about their experience in establishing a playgroup. The Association lady then asked us what our interest was and how we would constitute ourselves.

A woman named Helen came forward and said this was really important to her and she was prepared to commit herself to it. (The 'early adopter' or 'champion' – no, the 'champion' was the woman from the New King playgroup.) She had two young children and was looking for a safe, local environment for them to play in. I wondered what she did – or had done – for a living. Has the confidence of a professional about her.

Anyway, before you know it we're all arranging visits to the Association's toy library and weekly meetings in the Anglican Church Hall and it's all on. Never see Playgroup Assoc lady again. Which is as it should be for an 'enabler' role, I guess.

It makes such a difference expanding my occasional contact with other parents through chance playground meetings into the milieu of a structured group. There is an important management lesson in this. The creation of a group with 'permission' (legitimacy) and resources generates a whole new realm of creative mobility. This is Peter Senge in action!

It's also funny being the only male in a group like this. None of the women want to treat me as an oddity, and maybe it is just my own sensitivity to my gender in the context, but I am sure there is a sort-of circling of me – as if the women move around me, attentively but at a distance. Whereas they are quite comfortable moving through each others' spaces, and standing close to each other. They accept me easily enough when I behave in the same way – move in, talk, stand close, behave like them. But there is still a sense of curiosity and novelty about what brings one of me into their milieu.

Helen and Sharon are easier. Sharon lives just around the corner, so it's become natural to arrange to go down to the park together. She has only one daughter too, the same age as Rose. So Rose and Sharelle play and Sharon and I sit and natter. And then Helen drives across from a nearby suburb with her two kids. Maybe it's because we both have degrees and a level of articulation (Helen turns out to be a teacher), but Helen and I naturally seem to drift together. We have a similar macro-understanding of what it is to form and maintain groups, and how we want our children to learn etc. Helen's kids – Bronwyn and Rachel – have been over a couple of times to play in the family room, and Helen and I have 'taken tea'. Rachel is still only a baby really. I still get a buzz out of holding babies. Love that warm and cuddly bubbling saliva smell, and those neverending eyes.

It's good to find a use for the family room. Mei-ling and I had thought we would put friends in it when they came to stay, but it's remained pretty much the old mattress and packing crates it was when we moved in. Because you have to go onto the back veranda to get to it, it seems separate from the rest of the house. So Bronwyn and Rose delight in going in there and jumping up and down on the mattress. Take the old portable CD player in, pop on a Play School CD and they'll go for ages having a wow of a time.

And sitting watching kids play together makes chatting so easy. You just talk about whatever comes into your head. While away the time. I quite like the release of it.

Helen has been to look at a number of local schools. I think: already? But Rose will be old enough to start kindergarten next year, and onto primary school the year after that. A number of women at the play group already have their kids enrolled in private secondary schools! I can't believe the amount of planning these people are putting into child rearing. It's like the foundations are already dug and the piping ordered. I have not even considered this for Rose. I want her to develop as she determines as much as possible. And yet, of course, I'm already screening her exposure to commercial tv according to my own prejudices.

It's interesting, for instance, that Helen is prepared to drive all the way over to Westside Primary. As a teacher herself, she rates it very highly. I think we would've been interested in it too, as this was where Mei-ling and Jennifer workshopped Jennifer's production for Bower Bird. Unfortunately, according to Jennifer, the school is to close. Part of a government re-structure – smaller schools into bigger schools. Although of course all of the smaller schools to go are in migrant or disadvantaged areas. Payback for a recent industrial campaign by the teachers union, apparently.

Anyway, I was the one to deliver the bad news to Helen; which is ironic, that I as a newcomer should become a source of intelligence for a local. Helen wants to know more, but my source of information is a complex story and I'm not sure how far I want to go into it.

The fact is that in her first six months, Mei-ling has already publicly embarrassed the Education Minister. It seems a shame for her to lose an asset so early. Bower Bird was a reliable source of revenue, and had firm good will in the market place. Schools booked them up in a snap. But Mei-ling's ideological point is also valid from a business perspective: if Bower Bird is to continue to be sustainable as an income stream, Mei-ling cannot risk investment of company resources in work which is blocked at the eleventh hour by government intervention, particularly at the level of petty bureaucracy.

But she has created her own diversion. Even though she has publicly given the Education Department's officiousness (not in that word) as the reason for Bower Bird's demise, she has also announced a new program targeting the 18-25 year old age bracket – the upper end of what the funding bodies define as "youth".

This is exciting. No-one else is attempting it. Young adults are currently a massive gap in the local cultural tourism market. They go overseas as tourists of other cultures, but they don't see themselves as hosts to overseas cultural tourists back home. Mei-ling's aim is to draw them across the river from the pubs, casinos and gaming parlours into the Little Theatre at the Performance Centre – a gambit which pleases the Arts and Tourism Minister, we gather.

Mei-ling has commissioned Jennifer to research and write a performance-based promotion. Family Room is the working title – but only because she and Jennifer were there watching Rose bouncing away to a Play School tape at the time they conceived of the project. Mei-ling just had to have something to put on the grant application. It's that time of year again.

Ranald Whippet is running into production problems with the crew at the Performance Centre. It seems these high-flying city executives from the south can no better manage the insular insolence of performance venue staff than those who actually have frontline experience in cultural tourism. However, Phillipa is saying privately that the problem is Juneen; she isn't able to command the respect of the men in the crew – and that's most of them. They pretend not to hear, or claim she didn't say this or that, or do something else because they thought it was better. Yet there wasn't this problem on the previous promotion, which was designed and directed by Chamberlain and Hannah. So how come the two local gays get away with it, but the local lesbian production manager doesn't?

I don't think it's the female production manager at all. It's the outgrouping mentality described by Adorno *et al* in *The Authoritarian Personality*: in-group deviations from the norm are accepted before out-group deviations, according to a hierarchy determined by the in-group's dominant ideology. Geography is the stronger in-group marker here than sexual orientation. Does this mean gender is a weaker marker?

I keep marvelling, as I read all of this material on culture and organisations, personality and leadership, at Mei-ling's genius. Ironically, without De Leon around to posture and Wetherall (who has fled down south) to send poison faxes, there isn't much for anyone to complain about. Lillith Plant goes on from a presentation lead in Whippet's promotion to the creative direction role of her own in a cultural tourism promotion for rural Cooksland. And the Company is sending her to the National Tourism Workshop as its representative next month, just before she starts production. So she is constructively engaged in addition to her own business interests.

Meanwhile, subscriptions for the program of in-theatre promotions have already exceeded anything achieved by Malthorpe. Mei-ling bought Marketing and Sales a couple of magnums of bubbly when she heard. They all shared it after work last Friday. Even Rose had a sip! I was driving, of course.

*

71

Guttering

My father used to worry endlessly about the guttering of the houses he lived in. He would spend hours walking around the outside inspecting it, screwing up his eyes as if this would somehow aid his vision, because of course the houses were double storey and the gutters therefore far away. I never found out why he was so obsessed with them. I know he feared they would rust and water would run down the walls. This would lead to damp which would in turn lead to . . . I wasn't sure what. Shifting foundations, rotting window frames. But also a deep-rooted, historically inherited notion of health. If the water wasn't controlled from the roof down, channelled into storm-water systems and sewers, then there'd be rats and plagues and no end of misery. Not that he ever articulated it as such, but there was always this dark, foreboding undercurrent that ran through every gutter inspection. It was a serious business.

Of course, this was winter in Britain, where home ownership was hard to come by. But our first winter in sub-tropical King has rapidly brought gutters to my attention. Those outside the family room were blocked with leaves from the impressive array of trees that lined the perimeter of our compact our back garden, and with the near tropical rain storms we are getting here water pours liberally over the edges – both inside and outside – flooding the family room.

Luckily it was a Saturday, and Mei-ling and I had gone out onto the back veranda to enjoy the rain. We spotted the water streaming into the family room over the window ledge, and so were in there with towels and mops in reasonable time. I had to go out in my t-shirt and clean out the gutters. And because 38

Witherford Street comes off stumps from the side of an escarpment, I just needed to stand on a small set of steps at the back to reach them. I was soaked to the skin in seconds but, I quickly discovered, early winter storms in Cooksland are still in range upwards of 20 degrees Celsius.

Another reason, however, to proceed with the renovation of the family room. Mei-ling wants to move the kitchen down there. But then, she also wants a wardrobe built into the bedroom. And the veranda on the front of the house extended around the side to provide a car port also. And the quote we've had verges on over-capitalisation.

So now I've become a bit of a gutter-watcher too. Continually ducking out the back when it rains, to check on the leak-prone aluminium window and the gutters that fail it. As much for practical as for deeply superstitious reasons: the family room stinks when it gets damp, and the mattress takes ages to dry.

No guttering problems at the front of the house, thank goodness, because it's higher than the trees. It'd take more than a two-step stool to reach them! And anyway, the fronds of our lone palm tree thrash and slash in the rain, tossing up the streetlamp in wild knives of light like a madman in a circus riot, but they fall resolutely down when they're done and dead. Never up gutterwards.

Mei-ling and I both enjoy the palm. It reminds us once more of the old mental hospital in Singapore into which Bahasa Huayu Tamil were moved, when the company insisted they get the geomancer in because the palm tree outside Mei-ling's window represented bad *feng shui*.

Ironically, as the winter storms come to King, so Mei-ling has started to encounter them in the professional environment. A sponsorship deal for *The Rural Ward* has fallen through, for instance. Just as Lillith Plant flies off to Canberra for feedback on the project plan at the National Tourism Workshop, the special unit she was to have had access to at the Women's and Children's has virtually lost its rudder.

The Rural Ward is an interactive scenario set a country hospital threatened by closure. A proposal is on the table to save it: to make it into a regional centre for children and adults with disabilities who need special care during hospitalisation. The audience play the part of the local community, invited to a public meeting to save the hospital. But of course the central narrative is a vehicle for vignettes of all aspects of rural Australian life that find their way into the local hospital. Aussie battlers doing it tough. The Japanese and Chinese love this sort of stuff, and it reminds Americans where they came from. Mei-ling had negotiated access to the Women's and Children's special paediatrics unit so that the actors could observe real nurses on the job.

In a contra-deal, Phillipa and the new marketing executive, Alicia Driffield, had arranged a high-profile philanthropic sponsorship deal through Derek Barrimore's finance company, Asia Pacific Consulting. The sponsorship was to be split between the hospital and King's Company. (This is a high-risk promotion so Mei-ling, rightly, wanted a margin buffer.) Alicia was arranging a large reception at the opening in which hospital dignitaries and APC execs would meet some senior government ministers. Phillipa was calling on her political ties to see if they could even persuade the Premier and his wife to attend (Mrs Premier had, apparently, been a country nurse when she met the Mr Premier, who was a teacher in an Area School at the time, so there is good media mileage in it for them).

Unfortunately, like so many hospitals around the country under Managed Care funding arrangements, demand and an unseasonal late autumn flu have drained their budget, so they are looking for cost-cutting opportunities. According to Phillipa's contacts in the nursing union, a deeper reason the hospital does not want the attention King's Company will bring is that they have employed lay carers who are legally not accredited to administer the necessary medication. The hospital is actually placing them at personal risk of litigation in requiring them to do so. The last thing management want is a bunch of equally legally exposed performers thumping around the place drawing attention to the exposure.

So it's a mess. Apparently the hospital has been looking at ways of using Barrimore's money to keep the special unit open long enough to accommodate the Kings Company project - Phillipa and Alicia have been in negotiation with them for a couple of weeks, unbeknown to Mei-ling - but now the hospital has finally pulled the plug. Which leaves a King's Company Commission Member with egg on his face and the company, potentially, with a giant hole in its corporate profiling portfolio, its community partnerships program, and its budgeted income. Lillith Plant is not going to be impressed.

*

Wardrobe

We are experiencing a bit of a debacle over the installation of our wardrobe. We used the same builder who did the gate across the front porch. He came on Phillipa's recommendation, and did a good job on the porch gate, but he subcontracted the wardrobes. Understandably, Mei-ling is very specific about how she wants her built-ins to be. She imagines them in place, and in use, the way she imagines a set for a promotion when working with a

75

designer. And when "John the Chinaman", as the builder calls him, turns up to install the wardrobes, well they just weren't to specification.

I made the mistake of accepting delivery and partial installation, hoping that once they were in place Mei-ling would accept them anyway. But of course that was such a 'bloke' mistake. Don't make waves. Things will work out. Hope people will do the right thing but, when they don't, as long as it's not a major problem, we can put up with it. He's just doing his job, after all. A mate, etc.

Understandably, Mei-ling insisted the whole lot was taken away. She refused to have "John the Chinaman" back, demanded the builder re-build the robes himself (which he did) and we still have the long cupboard that was to have spanned the top of the two robes, to create the final "built in" effect, sitting in the study. I was embarrassed when "John the Chinaman" came back to collect his originals. I told him the builder was to finish them off, and he was to sort it out with him. He told me to fuck off in a very Chinese accent. Loss of face doesn't even get onto the starting blocks with this one.

Somehow, having spent so long in Singapore, I would've expected myself to deal with such situations better. I always tried to resist the "pushy foreigner" role, but in the end my own frustration would get the better of me, and face is so easy to break. And so easy for the Chinese Singaporeans to save if a "foreigner" is the cause. Yet here I am "back home" trying not to do any of that colonialist bullying stuff anymore, and the foreigner in our own land suffers by my passivity. Somehow a cross-cultural consultancy career is not looking promising, Masters or not.

On the subject of the thesis, Juneen has gone. It disturbs me that a member of the executive management team leaves so early on – they have barely been together eight months. For some reason Juneen seemed to wear a lot of Lillith Plant's ire for the shortcomings imposed on *The Rural Ward* production process by the withdrawal of the Women's and Children's. And there has been a cost overrun on the workshop move which Phillipa says a good production manager should have both anticipated and contained.

The plan is to eventually house the workshop in the Performance Centre, once the company moves into the Next Stage, and on-sell used wardrobe for profit, as the sets currently are. I have suggested to Mei-ling that she should combine King's Company's production team with Max Kingsbury's – it's more cost-efficient, and creates a functional relationship with the Performance Centre that might aid the strategic relationship Mei-ling needs. But she is understandably dubious about the surrender of autonomy that would accompany such a move. Kingsbury is already prevaricating about King's Company's residency status in the new venue. The production values of tourism promotion are very different from those of the performing arts, he says – of course!

But it was Mei-ling's decision to move the production and wardrobe facilities to temporary premises just around the corner. Integrate the off-site the production staff more with the on-site team. Plus the move has its symbolism. Enhancement of the production side of tourism promotion is crucial. Useful to show Max Kingsbury, just across the road, what's literally coming round the corner.

This makes the cost overrun as much Mei-ling's 'fault' as Juneen's. But Phillipa argues (in private) that it's Juneen's relationships with male staff that is the real root of the trouble –

both in the workshop and in production. The workshop move has apparently brought this to a head.

I can't help thinking Juneen is just being scapegoated because she is gay. Mei-ling doesn't need this type of shaving away of her executive team's solidarity at this still-early point. The group has been through the forming and storming stages and should now be performing. Once it falls open to this type of 'back door' incursion by the dominant (in this case out-) group, I am sure 'the blokes' will find other ways to invade and undermine the culture Mei-ling is striving to create. There is nothing blokes love more than a self-fulfilling prophesy, especially if it's the failure they always said and knew in their hearts would come. (Not that they personally will be in any way responsible. They did their bit. They tried. But what could they do? Etc.)

I'm nervous for Mei-ling in this. But I've discussed it with both Robert and Jennifer separately, and they seem to agree with Phillipa: Juneen is the problem. Perhaps I'm being over-analytical.

*

Rafters

The other thing my father used to worry about, apart from guttering, was heating. He was always the first up, downstairs to re-ignite the boiler from the embers of the night before. Warm the house up for the rest of us, generate some hot water for the morning washes most of us never had. I remember our back yard had a concrete coal bunker with two compartments – one for coal (for the fire) and one for coke (for the boiler). He always wanted to have central heating – and apparently did have it in his last house. And double-glazing – which was supposed to keep the cold out. And insulation, which was supposed to keep the heat in.

It seems ironic to me that I am installing insulation for the reverse reason – to keep the heat out. Having experienced our first King summer, and the distinct failure of our particular Cookslander breezeway (apparently we face the wrong direction to catch the evening sea breezes upon which the Cookslander cross depends), the preparation of some preventive measures for summer was called for. And having also experienced the first grips of the King winter, which can see the occasional chilly grab that walks through these weatherboard walls and floorboards like a ghost. And of course nobody ever designed a fireplace into the construction of these buildings. The sub-tropics was always assumed to be warm – which of course it was, compared to the original colonial motherland and the earlier colonies down south.

So we have had reverse-cycle ceiling fans installed in the two bedrooms and the study, and I have been up in the roof over the weekend laying insulation bats. Horrible job. You have to cover up as much of your body as possible. A complete face mask is recommended, but I wasn't prepared to fork out that much for something I would only use once. Nevertheless, I was decked out in safety goggles (the ones I use for whipper-snippering the back lawn), disposable safety masks, a cotton scarf wrapped around by head and tied behind my neck, garden gloves, and a full-length boiler suit tucked into thick socks and my old bushwalking boots. Rose barely recognised me.

Clumping up the ladder through the manhole into the roof all sounds are muted, and my movements encumbered. Felt like a moonwalker, but it's not me that's weightless, it's the glass-fibre (the reason for the protective clothing) batts. They seem to float in slow motion, I handle them so carefully. Because any fibres released into the house itself could, of course, get into Rose's orifices, eyes or skin and do untold damage. So I have to do the job when Mei-ling is around, to keep Rose away from the manhole (which, thankfully, is in the study). And I'm up there with a Stanley knife cutting and shoving as gently as I can, breathing into this muting synthetic barrier, feeling as insulated from the world as the stuff I am trying to lay. And I can't help thinking, isn't this a weird world we have created?

It is so hot up there, for one thing. And the closer you get to the eaves, the hotter and harder it gets to lay the batts. Yet at moments I am amazed at the ease of my acceptance of the environment. I used to climb trees as a kid and relish the breeze and views from the uppermost branches, invisible to all below. But being inside a roof is quite different. It's almost like being in a mausoleum, up amongst the rafters. I can remember the view of the attic cover in the ceiling of my grandmother's house, at the top of the stairs. It was black, and even blacker in the shadow of the stairwell and the hall beyond. It made me scared to ascend the stairs, as if ghosts and dark forces lay beyond that dense, light-absorbing square in an otherwise solid house.

So I've never found the prospect of rooves attractive, and never had cause to get up into one before. I'd always assumed they would be dark, and full of webs, spiders and rats. Whereas in reality the corrugated iron roof of a Cookslander is almost hospitable. Plenty of light seeps in through little holes here and there, and gaps between the sheets of iron, and where the roof meets the eaves. Very few webs and even fewer spiders. No rats at all. Even found a leak between corro sheets, which I was able to plug with some silicon.

Nevertheless, I get hot and irritable, and Mei-ling looks into the study sympathetically from time to time, urging me to come down for a cup of Jasmine tea or asking me how it's going. I can see an amused edge to her concern. She thinks it's funny to see this gruff man stomping around in the cotton wool of his own ineffectiveness. And I will appreciate the joke later.

Frankly, I am glad to see her amused by something. She is busily absorbed in planning at the moment. Sits on the bed surrounded with other people's travel brochures and cultural texts, consuming one after another (even though she has already read most of them several times over), trying to align in her mind the perfect combination of themes, styles, creative directors, and designers and the appropriate range of destinations to keep the local tourism factions happy, attract an audience, and enable the establishment of the core promotional team for the company.

If the Commission, and King, can be shown that there is enough work here for a base team, including talent, plus a broader palette of contractors, with her current at-the-door and pre-sale subscriptions record Mei-ling might just be in with a shot at a second contract. Six years here would give us enough investment in the house to make re-sale worthwhile, and would also see Mei-ling established enough back in Australia to move on to something else.

All of this depends, of course, on King's Company being able to demonstrate stronger domestic and international tourism in the state and, if possible, link this to cultural tourism. This is going to be most readily identifiable in rural events, but establishing rural initiatives takes longer due to the community development requirement.

Alicia Driffield's alignment with mainstream marketing isn't helping here. With the help of Derek Barrimore, she has Doherty's Stock and Feed just about signed up to sponsor a cutting-edge urban community project Mei-ling is planning with Dale Balanda's Cult Tourism. Great for King's Company, but how the urban disadvantaged and pastoral stock and feed go

81

together I'm not quite sure. Doherty's corporate profiling would surely have been perfect for a rural program, like *The Rural Ward*. I tell Mei-ling this – or rather I ask her whether it wouldn't be better if etc. – and I can see she listens, but it's just one idea in the mix with all of the rest.

There is a very strong introvert timbre to Mei-ling's intelligence, as well as a quiet passion. She can subtend a wide range of ideas and 'logics', and eventually out comes a decision or solution. It is extremely well thought through when it arrives, but she finds it impossible to articulate the intricacies of the argument while she is doing the thinking. I'm the reverse. Think with such an iron logic that I might as well be speaking aloud, it is so railroad straight.

Anyway, it can be frustrating being in the back seat is what I think I am telling myself. Dale Balanda has said he wants Robert to work as a consultant on the Diversity Project, as it has been dubbed. Far cry from the Tourism Australia Council, and administering a chamber orchestra darling, but nobody seems to bat an eyelid. It's okay for the boys, it seems. Again, even the gay ones, if they're 'local'. I shouldn't bitch about Robert. I like him. But surely even he would see how it looks. And would be aware of the power differential he and Dale can exercise, where Mei-ling could not on my behalf for instance.

*

Culture

It's nice to get out of the city. From Singapore, rural Malaysia was just a short drive across the causeway. But here, somehow, King is difficult to escape. Those sprawling suburbs that just roll lazily out from the city centre with an Australian drawl. But King's Company had scheduled a rural schools tour as an extension of *The Rural Ward* and, despite the total absence of Education Department approval and the withdrawal of the Women's and Children's Hospital support in King, there were dozens of regional centres anxious to buy it in.

Lillith Plant refused to do 'the regions', of course. So Mei-ling has used the old Bower Bird team as the talent and is on site for the first promotion herself. Juneen will oversee the remaining shows from here. (So Mei-ling has found a way of re-involving her with the company anyway! Is that the CEO's equivalent to an organisational wink?)

Jennifer has identified existing cultural tourism events on which each promotion will piggy back. In Wallaramulla, it's the annual spring agricultural show, which features a collection of slab huts the town has preserved, along with a local Chinese temple and market garden. They have built on the regular wood-chopping with shingle-splitting competitions, shingling demonstrations, long saw milling demonstrations, floor-board sanding and polishing demonstrations, slab-hut building, natural wax polish-making – a whole range of rustic and homespun building and renovation techniques that bring the home renovators out from King in droves. They even have the local Aboriginal community building humpies with the kids, in aid of the Wallaramulla Aboriginal Medical Service.

Jennifer has been here for a couple of weeks working with the kids in three area schools, to form the backbone of the historic re-constructions, and to take on major roles in the interactive segment, leading the 'visitors' in various arguments for and against the retention of the local hospital. She seems good at this. And of course the kids get into it so easily, commit to the 'dramatic action' of the scenario. And great to see them turn out in costumes their parents have painstakingly put together for them, often from photos in their own family albums. I have ideological misgivings about the exploitative nature of volunteerism, but when you see it in action in these country towns, there is no doubting its 'naturalness' and community power.

The promotion is a great success. The local show organising committee say it's the best 'feature event' they've ever had. And the fact that the hospital was adjacent to the showgrounds was an added bonus. The Company were even able to move the "protest" into the grounds of the hospital itself. All the more relevant as the Wallaramulla maternity service is under threat in reality!

For Rose, of course, it is her first contact with "the bush". And with real cows and sheep and pigs. I should've anticipated this better, built up to it more. Of course, we both did the "And you're going to see real cows!" stuff in the car, but nothing could prepare her for that giant wet nose suddenly appearing above her face, flanked by eyes almost the size of her fists, deep and black, but almond soft in shape, one ear flicking away the flies.

She staggered back, and I watched her face dealing with conflicting impulses to cry in fear and smile in wonder. But Mei-ling and I both quickly laughed and swept her up, and I held her at the same height as the cow and helped her pat its shoulder to feel how soft its fur was. Yes, she agreed, it was very soft. Couldn't get her to pat the sow, but. Much too smelly!

But she became really interested in mushrooms. They were everywhere in the lawn around the community hospital. She couldn't leave them alone, Touching them, stroking them, fingering them. Wanting to pick them but unsure whether it would be safe. I wasn't sure either at first. Could have been toadstools or any sort of poisonous fungus. Luckily the hospital's groundsman, a local council employee, spotted Rose and picked one for her. I checked with him that they were okay.

"Sure are, mate. Here, take a couple back to the city with yer. That'll give yer neighbours something to think about."

Actually dug me up a small patch complete with the soil in which they had grown, so that I could replant it back home. He was a lovely old bloke – could've been part of the 'action' of the promotion, old dungarees, flannelette shirt, battered hat. Winked at me as he invited Rose to take some mushrooms for herself from his cupped hands.

She has great capacity for emotion, Rose. At one point in *The Rural Ward* the kids are looking after a young boy who is dying of starvation during the Depression, bringing him things like a pair of shoes (because he has none) and some damper their mum has cooked or a rabbit their dad has trapped, and the local Chinese community bring herbal medicines (actually the kids of the local Chinese restaurateur, who is from Singapore). Rose was in tears, and then clapped for joy when the boy recovered enough to take a sip of broth.

The real tourists lapped it up. It was easy to pick out those who were from overseas, and they were in their dozens. Which must be a reflection on the success of Mei-ling's strategic leadership, because Malthorpe did hardly any regional work during his time.

Poor Robert looked lost. Awkwardly hanging around and smiling at people a lot. Not quite sure what to do at a country show. Not quite confident around the animals. A sort of distant gay interest in the manly pursuits of wood-chopping and shingling, and wattle-and-daub. And merging not-quite-inconspicuously into the crowd for *The Rural Ward*. Wondering what he had gotten himself into, he said. He's supposed to be gaining some sort of 'work experience' for his role on the Diversity Project as 'dramaturg'. Says he's still got no idea what one is. I was afraid I couldn't help. No, he said, I'm not surprised. And at least we shared a laugh.

So interesting to watch a man who seems so 'endemic' in the city environment and yet, out here in the supposed heartland of Australian culture, is so clearly out of place.

*

Study

There is something rather impressive about study, and having a dedicated room in which to do it. In Singapore, because our apartment was so small (well, they all are there), I had a desk in the bedroom. And that is something I have often done – as a student, as someone sharing a house with others – where I sleep and where I study or work have been one in the same.

When I first met Mei-ling she had a separate space she used to call the office. I guess that was because she had been living with a guy who ran a business from home, complete with computers and accounting systems and separate phone and fax lines - even a photocopier. But now that we have bought our own home for the first time, it has separate a study. And while Mei-ling has her own desk, I have pretty much the run of the space. Especially at the moment, as I have piles of notes and books everywhere – neat little piles for transmittal back to the Uni, in order of return. And notes from the coursework, in neat distance learning modules, stacked systematically around the edges of the room.

It is just as well Mei-ling has an entire work-space *at work* to spill into. It means that at home she is happier to spread her work

86

around her on the bed – be it preparation for a promotional event, a campaign, or choosing an annual program of the two. The one seems to have merged into the other recently – I don't know what the final program for next year is, but is has been replaced by endless texts on *A Midsummer Night's Dream* and the cultures of South East Asia. She has great ambitions for this her first real creative event for King's Company. She wants it to involve the dance and music from each tourist destination in the region, whilst remaining true to the structure of Shakespeare's story, so that she will succeed in attracting both a cultural tourism audience and a performing arts audience. A vital step in her change strategy as well as, of course, her first real act of public profile.

Anyway, it means that we are both 'studying' in our respective ways, at home at the same time, me in my (oops, *our*) study, and Mei-ling in the bedroom, with Rose alternating between us. Me at the antique but work-a-day desk Mei-ling bought me for my birthday, elbows akimbo, book open in front of me – perhaps a notepad and pencil to the side. I still love the cleanness of a freshly sharpened lead. The sense of preparing for the task each time. And no messy blue or black blobs from bad biros. Just soft, grey strokes upon a clean sheet of paper.

I'm hopeful that Rose does not see this as 'being ignored'. I'm hopeful that she inscribes this as a positive role image: her mother and I, in separate rooms, both focusing on the act of study, each in our different ways. And it does seem to be working. I came out this morning wondering why I hadn't heard Rose for a while, and found her laying on the floor before a dormant t.v. with a book open in front of her, telling herself its story as if she were 'reading'.

I'm very conscious of visibly 'using' the computer for Rose's sake. It's true that the computer has transformed the act of study for me. These days I do all of my writing on the screen. But I can't develop my thoughts in the first place without the books, and the desk, and me sitting at it, pencil in hand.

I get this from my mother, of course. My father knocked back a scholarship to grammar school to go out and get a job. A collection of Reader's Digest was about all he left behind in terms of books. And even then, I couldn't be sure he ever read them. Yet as I read I think of him so often. Trying to understand still, I suppose, somebody so totally unlike me in a world in time and place so different to mine, and yet who I find within myself more and more each day.

There is his intellect, for instance. He never was one to mince his ideas. Unlike me, who struggles to tease them apart and make sense of them with my railroad logic. Dad used to just make the observation or announce the conclusion, and it always seemed so incisive, so insightful. So, still not as bright as my old man, even though a degree-and-three-quarters better qualified.

I wonder if that's a myth. Robert reckons it is. Born and bred in Australia, he still sees his old man. Even though his father is a professional, he says the perception of a father's intelligence is always over-rated by the son. The Oedipus Complex Meets Male Cognition, he calls it. I like Robert's mind. He always seems very clear in his lack of clarity. I don't know that I understand mine. I don't think I handle uncertainty very well.

*

Government

Howard Way has made the most amazing gaff. And what's worse, he seems to be getting away with it. Dan Forrest has been making a whole series of public statements about the War on Terror recently, and Way has as always been in step behind him, as if Australia is some dutiful child of our mighty Ally. Given the number of times Prime Minister and Mrs Way have stayed with President and Mrs Forrest at their ranch, you would have thought Way would've understood him better. Anyway, the day after Forrest made an impromptu comment about the 'threat of ter-r-r-r-rism on our dar-r-rsteyyep' on one of those 'doorstops' just before he boards the helicopter on the White House lawns, Way is making a major pronouncement about the threat of tourism (sic) on Australian shores.

The press immediately jumped on him: wasn't tourism one of Australia's major economic drivers? Wasn't it the central plank of the government's regional infrastructure policy? Etc. Yes, Way replies, but it is unwise of Australia to sink all of its eggs into the one basket. We should not be overly dependent on an economic driver that is so subject to fickle market forces in the near region. Meaning Asia of course. I still remember Way tickling the Immigration trout when he was Treasurer, applauding the withdrawal of Business Migration because it was only bring Asian migrants into the country anyway, rather than creating work for 'Australians'. And here he is on the news, once again shoving just so many feet into his mouth.

It wasn't half-an-hour later, in his next interview, that he was back-pedalling like mad, and with just as many feet in his mouth. On 2FS (national broadcaster), yes of course tourism is important, but it is also easy for terrorists to enter Australia on tourist visas, disguised as tourists. It was a major border security issue, he said. And (and this is the danger for Mei-ling) the dependence of rural

Australia on cultural tourism exposed them to such terrorists – a country event was an easy target, and easy to penetrate.

Forrest came from his bed in the middle of the night, apparently, to defend his 'invailyooerble Osschraylyun ferreynd', to confirm that 'wi awl hayd t' bi warchf'l erv the trayd iern ter-r-r-rism thert kerd bi fercilleetayded bah tour-r-r'sts.' An hour later Way's Tourism Minister was announcing a Senate review of the relationship between tourism and terrorism. Talk about a ball rolling!

*

Bearers

I have picked the wrong time to chuck a fruity, and have to find a way of apologising. The trouble is, Mei-ling doesn't ask for apology. But once I have thrown up one of my rare but effective manly flounces of anger, Mei-ling can be difficult to reach. It's easy to say it's a face thing. No matter how much we may vary from our parents due to the ideological milieu in which we separate out from them, one of the things I'm learning from Rose is just how much is absorbed beyond words, and before words, that is central to the way we manage ourselves in relation to our deeper emotions. And if Mei-ling inherited a vestige of 'face' from her parents, then I inherited the equivalent from my English parentage. In fact, Mei-ling is much better than me at being in contact with and working from an emotional authenticity. But anger is one emotion we have both learnt to express only with the most dire imagined consequences. We equally avoid it at all costs.

The fear at the centre, however, is different. My fear is loss of control. I fear a violence resulting from my anger which I have been brought up to believe will be futile and ineffectual, even destructive. Whereas for Mei-ling it is loss of love. So I have to re-assure her that I love her. But without reacting, again in my own anger, to any surface responses from Mei-ling the Adult, which will address the presenting content of my outburst at face value. Predictably, with disdain. In other words, I have to take it back, and then take it.

Perhaps it is my growing sense that I will not complete my thesis this year, and it will drag on into next year and another set of university fees. I feel the pressure of my own professional prospects dragging out into a disappearing future. And somehow the endless piles of washing, sorting on the bed, and sessions hanging it out under the house, have become a focus for my anxiety – the drudgery of endlessly folding and re-folding, packing things away in draws only to unpack them, wash them after use, and re-sort them for packing once more, the opening and closing of drawers – it has just been getting me down.

And increasingly I end up down hanging up washing either during Rose's naps (when I should be studying) or, on nights when Mei-ling is late back or in at the theatre, after Rose has gone to bed, because I haven't gotten around to it during the day and the washing up has beckoned and I have not wanted to short-change Rose and on it goes. So I give up time for Rose (as I should), and the washing waits.

I thought I had solved this one, by hanging a plastic swing from Big W from one of the bearers under the house, and creating a bit of a sandpit down there, so that Rose could play while I hung out washing during the day. But this is working less and less, as Rose's attention span does not last out the "hang". So I try to do it in shifts or fit it in when Rose is asleep – and even then I am tense because I am trying hard to listen for her waking.

Anyway, tonight it just all became too frustrating, and I was down there when Mei-ling and Phillipa came home, their faces entering the dull yellow glow of the one naked bulb with "Hi, I'm home" smiles. And I was terse and sulky and self-absorbed, and did not notice the strain behind Mei-ling's eyes or the lines around Phillipa's face. Just cursorily asked them if they had had tea – which was, of course, a pointed comment, because it was unlikely that they would have but I had prepared ours a couple of hours ago and no-one had come home to eat it and here I was still "working" on these mindless, worthless, unrewarding tasks and would anyone like a drink because I certainly would – all attitude, of course. Unspoken. All pointed, loaded words withheld.

So Mei-ling asks what's wrong. And I say nothing. And she says it doesn't seem like nothing. So I mumble ineffectually about being sick of hanging washing out at 8 o'clock at night because I haven't gotten around to it during the day. Mei-ling says she will hang the washing out, and she and Phillipa set about it cheerfully, chatting to each other and giggling. And that makes me even angrier. Back up in the house, finalising meal preparations for serving. Opening a bottle of wine. Paying Mei-ling out when she comes up looking for me by withholding and hiding in my anger some more. Just so effective.

And when I eventually ask her how her day was, I learn bit by bit, over the meal, through conversation between her and Phillipa mostly, that today she had her first formal meeting with the Minister for Tourism and the Arts, Doug Dingwall, and Max Kingsbury, and King's Company Commission member Harold Winterbourne (in his Cooksland Tourism and the Arts departmental role), to discuss the Next Stage occupancy. The Minister begins by describing it as Mei-ling's jewel, the jewel in

King's Company's crown, as if the company would be as the Minister and the Premier had promised, resident in the Performance Centre's new medium-sized theatre.

But as the unveiling of the architect's model for the theatre proceeded, so the seating requirements Mei-ling had prescribed to the Minister and Kingsbury three months earlier become a point of discussion. Kingsbury and Dingwall talk to each other as if Mei-ling isn't there, about the requirements of the "other users". By which, of course, Kingsbury means King's performing arts companies and performing arts ventures from interstate and overseas. Mei-ling intervenes: of course King's Company will allow other companies into the theatre. It is as much to their advantage as it is to the government's and to the Centre's to be seen to be collaborating and working with members of the performing arts community as well as travel agencies and tour operators. That was the whole point of the tourism-led sustainability strategy for the arts.

So then Kingsbury actually presents the question: So how many weeks a year does King's Company wish to book the theatre then?

It's such a game. Mei-ling says that she doesn't understand the question. King's Company will be happy to take booking enquiries from anybody and work around and in with them accordingly. The coordination of both sectors, tourism and the arts, needs to be in King's Company's hands. How else can it model the economic benefits to the arts of integration between the two industries?

Ah, but this is perhaps where they may be some misunderstanding, says the Performance Centre's Chief Executive Officer, for the Performance Centre's role is to *manage* the new theatre for government. It is to be *part* of the Performance Centre.

And the Centre itself needs the flexibility of this new theatre for other *commercial* opportunities that may come its way. There are costs to recover, after all.

So Kingsbury is clearly resisting the central thesis of the King's Company strategy: that the arts is commercially unsustainable without government subsidy. Kingsbury is the arts entrepreneur, the arts impresario, who will ensure the Performance Centre is commercial viable for government. The arts do not need tourism dollars.

Unspoken, of course. And it's natural to expect resistance to change. But Mei-ling's strategy is one of government initiation, and government needs to lead the charge. Dingwall needs to be pointing out to Kingsbury where his government stands, and why; the expected outcomes of the Next Stage/King's Company strategy; the leadership role this will give Cooksland in Australia, and internationally. Instead, Dingwall continues to pander to Kingsbury, playing into his little 'days of occupancy' game.

To her credit, Mei-ling doesn't pull any punches. She makes it clear that for King's Company to be "resident" in title only is not what was promised, and does not meet the government's needs. The advantages of being a resident company include unrestricted access to the stage, for creative development, for instance, or rehearsal with parts of set during construction for assessment purposes, holding launches and sponsorship opportunities at the company's convenience in their own venue, and generally having a "property" in which to invest and to exploit the commercial and corporate advantages of its public identification with.

This is in addition to the vital role the company needs to play in bringing together tourism and arts industries in contiguous and joint activities that will demonstrate the economic benefits of integration to the arts industry. It is essential that King's

Company move 'out' of office space associated with a government tourism commission and into a performing arts space that sets the stage, so to speak, for government's strategic change in arts and tourism funding and profiling.

But Kingsbury and Dingwall persist, and in the end Mei-ling says that King's Company will require the theatre for 48 weeks in the year, and will provide a full calendar of occupancy, will negotiate with any other performing arts company as well as tour operator or promoter who might wish to hire the space. Indeed, collaboration will remain entirely *in* the question, as planned. She then sat through another couple of hours of unnecessary (at her level of authority) discussions about fire exits, toilets and so forth, knowing she hasn't heard the last of this. Just when you think you have firm foundations, they try to hang you from the bearers.

I immediately asked if this seeming vacillation from Dingwall was a state government reaction to the Howard Way 'tour-r-r-rism' gaff. But Phillipa, who has worked as an adviser to Dingwall in the Department of Tourism, says it's just him all over. It's more likely he is just caving in to pressure from Kingsbury.

Anyway, that was the last event in Mei-ling's day. So she and Phillipa arrived home in desperate need of a debrief. And, fortunately, were able to provide one for each other during the meal. And then Phillipa leaves and Mei-ling crashes into bed, reassuring me that she will hang the washing out in the future. And I excuse myself, saying I have just a bit of study to finish up. And am now here, feeling like a right shit.

*

Picture Rail

It was a day of odd conversations today. Robert Cunningham has left messages a couple of times saying we should get together again, so I asked him to come round and help me hang some of our paintings. Almost a year since our return to Australia, and they are still lying around propped up against walls. One of the features of the house that had finally 'sold' Mei-ling was the picture rail around the lounge – something we've never had before. She was excited about the prospect of finally hanging our cross-cultural assortment of pictures properly. Even treated herself to some brass picture rail hangers early on. I've been wanting to surprise her with the completed job for ages – even secretly bought the lengths of brass chain - and now seemed as good a time as any, with Max Kingsbury fomenting his resistance to the state government's (and Mei-ling's) combined tourism and arts strategy, might just cheer her up.

Getting round to such a job in a way that involves Rose is difficult, because it means standing on step ladders and chairs and having my back to the lounge etc. I also thought hanging paintings would be an aesthetic activity we 'blokes' could enjoy together. And I hoped Robert could help out keeping Rose occupied. Although inviting him in the afternoon, she might just take her nap and let us get on with it.

In the event, she didn't. She was excited at having a visitor in the house. So we shared the load, involving her as much as possible in the process of choosing spots to hang the pictures, handing up the hooks for us to hang on the rail, telling us whether the picture is 'right' of not. And at one point, of course, she just had to take him out into the back garden to show him the mushrooms, which have indeed taken splendidly as the groundsman from Wallaramulla predicted. I went out to relieve him, but he was quite happy squatting down with Rose over the sizeable patch of burgeoning round-topped fungi, asking her questions about them, where they came from, and yes, he was there too, did she remember? Wasn't a nice place etc. Very easy and not at all the 'displaced person' he seemed at Wallaramulla itself.

He also turns out to be quite an expert on architecture. Conjectures that the picture rail is not an original feature of the house, because it extends seamlessly around the entire lounge, whereas the lounge was originally built as two rooms off a central hallway. Internal walls have since been removed.

As we progressed, Robert asked me how I thought Mei-ling was going? "Fitting in" was the term he used. He said it must be challenging for her to return to Australia, having been 'out of the culture' for so long. I said I thought that was true, but she had been more 'out of the culture' in Singapore. In a sense, she was 'returning to culture', and with a mandate for 'culture change'. Her entire organisational and industry 'brief' was cultural in nature. As an agent of change, there was an inherent alterity to the role.

He agreed, but wondered whether I understood just how much antagonism there was to that mooted change. Everyone in the Cooksland tourism industry was aware of the plan, but the performing arts industry were only just starting to understand its implications. He said Mei-ling needed to communicate the message far more widely and forcefully if she was going to succeed.

I explained she was limited by staffing and resourcing, and by the body of existing operations she had inherited. He must be aware of the magnitude of the challenge, having turned down a role in the company. I also pointed out that the plan was to model by action rather than by propaganda.

He asked me if I really knew what I was talking about. It was quite confrontational, and he knew it immediately. Tried to withdraw the challenge in it by redefining: did I understand what "the arts" meant to the performing artists in King? Had I had much to do with "the arts"?

I had to admit I hadn't, apart from the community arts, which formed a natural ideological synergy with cultural tourism. I mean, I went to the theatre, and attended concerts, but as a consumer. I'd always thought of the arts from a sociological perspective, I suppose. As a function of its source of patronage. Businessmen like to see the competitive individual they are transformed into alongside the creative being they know they should be but can never achieve. They like to see the talent they can never find within themselves fostered in its purest form, in the artist.

Similarly, government sees artists as the expression of intellectual and emotional freedom they can never allow themselves – politicians with their need to constantly keep their feelings and expressive selves at the behest of political imperative, bureaucrats forever bound by the need for process, fairness and accountability.

So the arts are a reflection of society, in that sense. But in the sense of society's aspiration to a perfection it can never achieve. Keeping the myth alive, as it were.

So not, said Robert pointedly, staring at me with a slightly inclined head so that he appeared to be looking up at me, as the actual highest point of consciousness of their time?

I thought he was joking at first. I almost laughed. Certainly started to smile.

Because that's how they see themselves, he continued. As the expression of social consciousness and conscience. They see themselves as separate from and superior to base concerns like business and politics. They see this forced alliance with a commercial enterprise as crass as tourism immensely insulting. And the community arts you talk of, even though I know it was highly professional in its time, they think of as amateur. So can you see the magnitude of the challenge Mei-ling has to overcome?

There was an awkward pause, in which I didn't know what to say. I knew Robert had run a chamber orchestra but I hadn't really thought of him as 'part' of the arts world. I couldn't tell whether he was defending them.

I'm not one of them, he said, as if reading my mind. I've just worked *with* them. So I know how they think. But you can see why I have reservations about joining Mei-ling's enterprise just now.

I nodded, and told him I hadn't thought about it in that way, but could understand what he was saying. I'm not sure now whether my next gambit was an attempt to regain an upper hand or a clumsy attempt at empathy, but I asked him if that was why he felt so out of place in Wallaramulla. It was that obvious, was it? he said with a self-amused cross between a grimace and a grin. But no, he said. He wasn't feeling for the 'death of the arts' or anything like that. It was more for the people themselves. The locals. That they had to reduce themselves to this.

To what? I asked. I know the theory, he said: cultural tourism brought communities together - and, I chipped in, unlike community arts, gives them a new economic future. Yes but this is their culture, he said. It's their way of expressing their identity, what binds them as a community. Must they commodify their very soul in the interests of economic viability? It just seemed to ... I don't know, so sad, he said. Sorry David, I know it's Mei-ling's life's work and ... it just seemed sad.

Anyway, he said, trying to change the subject and jolly himself along, How was I coping? Because I was very much in a new culture, wasn't I, as primary carer? And suddenly the focus had turned to me. And he was right. I am now very much in a mothers' culture. A woman's culture. I guess, I said, I am politically interested in exploring that side of myself, just as I'm interested in exploring alternative management structures to the patriarchal in my thesis work with Mei-ling and King's Company.

Robert said he could identify with that, because he very much took on the woman's role in his relationship with Dale. At the same time as taking on the intellectual role. So he found himself subtending the two internal imperatives – one a highly patriarchal intellectual role, the other the emotional or feeling intelligence of the woman in a relationship. He wondered if I had ever thought about my own sexuality. I said I hadn't. But of course, now I have! ie. by virtue of our conversation.

So, a confronting conversation, but one I enjoyed. For Robert was not himself confrontational. The content was, and I was interested in the new thoughts it evoked. And I enjoyed him, the way he took risks. Found him readily engaging. *Liked* him. Anyway, we didn't get much further because Phillipa turned up. Robert had told her where he was going, so she came round to view progress, and with some flowers to add to Mei-ling's surprise. It was a lovely gesture.

She inspected our choice of paintings and positions – it was like a viewing at a gallery. Then she played with Rose while Robert and I finished the last couple. He had to go then, so Phillipa gave him a lift. But while he was saying his farewells to Rose, and having a last little play with her, she walked me to the front door and told me about her latest psychological project with her therapist: her desire to have children – which she both has and doesn't have.

She fears the dependence, it seems, but strongly desires the relationship (with a child). It has been suggested, she said, that she should spend more time with children she feels for, and something she was going to suggest to us was that she takes Rose out on Sunday mornings as summer comes on. She could take her swimming or out to the park, or just out. It is something she would enjoy, and it would give Rose exposure to people and places other than Mei-ling and myself, and would give us a morning together – to lie in or 'whatever' – with ever that amber glint in her eye.

I said this was a generous offer, and she seemed pleased, but I get the odd sense, at the back of my brain, of somebody denying herself one experience – sexual intimacy with someone of the opposite sex – in order to have another – an intimate relationship with a child – as if the two are mutually exclusive. And I wonder why she has chosen to approach me with this proposition rather than Mei-ling. Perhaps I've taken on the 'mother' role more completely than I had imagined!

With that they both left. Robert even gave me a gentle hug and a peck on the cheek. And as I write this, I am left with the feeling that this afternoon both friends have hung quite personal issues in the 'gallery' of our lounge in a way that Mei-ling will never see, amidst the paintings themselves. The irony is that Rose has chosen now to finally settle for a nap. And I should be taking the opportunity to prepare for dinner, so that the house is ready with a meal and surprise for Mei-ling.

*

Well, the surprise worked. Mei-ling and I made love tonight. She is now sleeping restfully. It's nice to see her at peace for a change.

*

Bathroom

I was at Sharon's yesterday. Rose and Sharelle were having a play in the sandpit. We were planning with Helen to do a trip to the riverside artificial beach at South Bank, but then Rachel was sick so Helen had to take her to the doctors and this was the fall-back plan.

Sharon was showing me their new bathroom. I said we were planning to re-do the rear end of our house, including the bathroom, and they had just refurbished theirs' so … It was while we were in there, and caught sight of ourselves in the mirror, that Sharon chose to tell me she was pregnant. I enthused and congratulated her and checked with her that it was what she wanted – and was genuinely pleased for her. But it was the way she told me, looking into the mirror at me, eyes dropping as her head turned to face me then engaging my eyes directly. "I've got some news." A pause. "I'm pregnant." With a slightly coy smile.

It was as if she was confessing something to me in secret. And more than that, something she feared might be a betrayal. As if we had been lovers, but this would put an end to it. And the choice of the bathroom as the location. I mean, perhaps it was just coincidence, but there was an intimacy implied, a distinctly sexual timbre to the revelation.

I know I have found Sharon attractive. More so than Helen, for instance. So this could just be my projection. But when Sharon has spoken about her relationship with her husband before, and how it started, she has done so with a real sense of herself as being at the centre of desire in it. He very much sought her out, despite pressure from his own family to marry into ethnicity (he's from a large Italian family). She was talking about him moving down the coast against his family's wishes, and I asked her why he did that, and she said pointedly "Me", with an emphasis on the "m", and that same direct eye contact.

It leads me to wonder whether I am seriously immune to awareness of sexual interest by others in me. When I was younger, and a bit of a root rat, I always knew it was I who pursued sexual interest, and that was what resulted in sex. My own determination. I had no sense ever of responding to sexual desire in me from someone else. It was not until Mei-ling and I were well and truly together that she confided she had longed for me from the moment we first met. Whereas my first contact with Mei-ling was purely professional, as a freelance journalist, doing a story on Surrey Street. Through the first interview over lunch, and a series of follow-up contacts to check details, I was just working. It wasn't until she rang to thank me for the final article, when it turned up on her desk in print, that my thoughts turned to a potential relationship.

Then Mei-ling became unlike any other relationship I had ever had. Once we started to meet socially, it just sort of 'took' me. I was compelled to see her, to ring her, to seek her out, not by lust or ego but by some unseen force I couldn't quite put my finger on. It's the nearest I think I've ever come to thinking there might be something in the idea of God. As if our souls came together in some parallel ether in which spirits hurtle around like meteors until they collide and entangle and are from thence joined forever. That is how it has been for Mei-ling and I. Fell out of the meteor shower together, and have travelled together through the ether ever since. Fish on land.

Since that time all I've been aware of really, in terms of sexual attraction, is me diverting those I feel for other women. Not even out of guilt. More out of a sense of: well, it's irrelevant really; I'm with Mei-ling, and I don't want to be with anyone else. Which is why the exchange in Sharon's bathroom interested me so much. The possibility. The chance. But one even now I know I have no intention of pursuing and, frankly, could just have imagined. But why would I?

What interests me even more is that it wasn't Sharon I had an arousing, erotic dream about last night. It was Helen. All she did was come to the front door, but it was as if there was an entire story behind her advent there. She had come because it was inevitable we would have an affair. She was flushed, slightly breathless in her own ingenuous way. Unable to resist the inevitable any longer. I could imagine the softness of her breasts under her t-shirt, her nipples warm and inviting, rising and falling with her lungs. She had come to confront me with our love. To fall into my arms.

She did not know how she was going to say it. I knew, immediately I opened the front porch door to her, what she had come for, and that my feelings matched hers. I did not know what I would say to Mei-ling. Wondering if it was at all possible to have the affair and keep it from her. It would be so natural to sleep with Helen. So unavoidable. In the way it had been with Mei-ling so many years before.

But it wasn't the sexual attraction I thought I divined from Sharon. There was no lust. It was love. And the need to express this bodily.

I wish I understood Jungian psychology better. I'm sure I would make a better fist of understanding this if I did. Organisational psych is just so *behavioural* by comparison. I'll be glad when I can stop reading it.

*

Veranda

It's a strain having the Lees here. Just when things were looking up. Mei-ling needed all of her energy for *Dream*. She has succeeded in developing a working relationship with Kendall Chamberlain and, thanks to Robert Cunningham's contacts in the world of chamber music, found the brass quartet she wanted for live music onstage. She has also found a few local circus performers. And is successfully marketing it as a Christmas spectacle, for all the family.

I'm really looking forward to seeing it. Mei-ling has chosen to set it in a turn-of-the-century colliery town on the East Coast of Australia, hence the brass and circus performers. Just coming out of a depression. Union movement decimated by a coalition of industrial muscle and private enterprise-oriented government, but the unions on the verge of a comeback because people have had about as much as they can take.

This world, which is the world of what I am informed they call the 'mechanicals' in the original Shakespearean version, is unknowingly situated in a magical world of older, deeper, 'magical' cultures: not only Australia's Aboriginal cultures, but also the worlds of the Bahasa speakers of Indonesia and Malaysia to the north, and Chinese to the Northwest, the Tamils to the West, and the Polynesians and Melanesians to the Northeast and

East. The lovers in the Shakespeare play are young Australians of today thrown back in time. It's a great concept. She is even using some of the original Shakespearean text, and bits of Mendelssohn's music (somewhat 'rocked up').

Tristan Malthorpe's return to town for the Spring promotion was dull by comparison. He held his usual soirees with local supporters – a bit like Arte de Leon, holding court, offering work 'Down South' to young locals. It's unbelievable the extent to which Sydney and Melbourne still think they are 'it'. But perhaps that's how Malthorpe sustained his professional identity here all that time: with the promise of the world beyond. That's tourism, I guess.

Mei-ling has now had her first profile in the press. A features writer with the Herald has finally understood that Mei-ling is the first woman in Australia to fill a position like this, and that she is also the first Australian in the tourism industry to run a national tourism company in Asia, has links in the region and – goodness! Could this be a story???

But she is finding it hard returning to the hands-on role of creative director on a promotion here. All the while we were in Singapore, Mei-ling spoke about Australia as if that was the cornucopia of all that was professional in cultural tourism, the mould into which she hoped to pour BHT. And she succeeded. When she left, BHT was the national flagship for Singapore in SE Asia, with well-received tours into Malaysia, to Hong Kong, and Beijing, and strong professional links resulting.

As she talks now about the disparateness of performance styles amongst the talent on *Dream,* and childishness and attention-seeking behaviours of some of the more traditional actors, the inconsistencies in experience and training – the way Mei-ling describes her working day in rehearsal it sounds like a constant exercise in the role-switching described in leadership theory. But whereas most leaders switch roles within well-defined organisational parameters – the meeting with clients, the meeting with the executive team, the meeting with the Commission, the meeting with the workers or staff – Mei-ling is doing it all within the one environment of the rehearsal, moment to moment. First one spot fire, then another, each performer reacting off the other as well as Mei-ling AND the scenario. Sounds like barely controlled chaos.

And this is the 'creativity' from which business is supposed to be learning! Robert may be right; these people may see themselves as the 'highest point of consciousness in their time', but they behave like overgrown children. Perhaps the true meaning of innocence! If I were Mei-ling, I would be re-thinking the 'transformation' I was strategically leading. Who wants the performing artists if this is what they are like up close?

The irony is that it makes the BHT process look gold standard. The talent for promotional events there were determined, concentrated, worked together, took to ensemble processes like it was going out of style, understood the value of the strategic enterprise they were part of, and had a will to make the whole work. It never occurred to me at the time, but I've wondered since whether it was a face thing – nobody could be seen to let the others down or to falter at the fence, as it were. Whereas back here in good old individualist Australia, it is every man and woman for themselves – they are all in there for their slice of the love and rapture and attention. Give me ticketing agents any day, Mei-ling despairs; at least they get on with the job.

And perhaps that is the achievement of the Ranald Whippets and Tristan Malthorpes of the world – to stand back far enough to craft the exteriors and allow the individuals to fight it out amongst themselves. To let "the promotion" or "the tour" get on with itself, and just be there at the end to claim the concept, claim the structure, claim the overall success. "Everyone has such a *wonderful* time!" Perhaps there is no place for collectivism and consensus in a culture like ours.

We had a quiet moment to ourselves on the front verandah the other night, as the sun was setting and the Lees were putting Rose to bed. I asked Mei-ling about the 'highest point of consciousness' argument that Robert put, and whether this was something we had not taken into account. She said that she had, actually. There wasn't the same sense of the arts as profession in Singapore, that was true, because arts there was more culture as an expression of identity rather than culture for profit or commerce, for consumption.

The 'highest point of conscious' discourse is the same back here, she said; it is an expression of the artist's identity. But, she reminded me, the Surry Street alliance *was* with a community arts movement driven by an ideology of social change. There is no 'highest point' of consciousness in either cultural tourism or community arts; its consciousness is consensual. That is its strength. An arts fraternity locked into 'highests' in 'consciousness' is still yoked to the hierarchic, competitive ordering of patriarchal discourse.

So Robert may be right, but King's Company's task is to bring the city's performing arts talent to a new sense of identity, a new perception of their role in the community. Her faith, she says, remains in the fundamental humanity of the arts fraternity in King, as it is in the tourism community. Extend a share in the arrangements of power and control, as a matter of practice, and eventually participants will see that there is an alternative mode of operation that does not require individual competition and survival of the fittest. People will understand what many businesspeople actually believe, that economy can be both profitable and benefit all parties.

It is re-energising to be reminded of why we are doing this. I admire the clarity and cogency of Mei-ling's mind in moments like this. Such a vision of the bigger picture, the game plan.

Anyway, I guess we'll see when *Dream* finally hits the stage, because if it's one thing Mei-ling can do it is, like the Whippets and Malthorpes, create an external conceptual framework strong enough to carry the production regardless. It would be ironic, however, if BHT proves in the end to have been the best of it and, in reality, a state tourism commission in Cooksland is in fact a professional step down.

Against this backdrop, the added pressure of having to service her parents really isn't helpful. Within two days of their arrival in King, Mei-ling's mother made the usual loving but slightly hurt comments about Mei-ling's name. And before you know it, Mei-ling is dutifully sitting on the sofa with her mother, pouring over a book of Chinese names and characters, listening to her mother bemoan how much nicer the characters used to look in the version of her name with which she was christened.

I know that inwardly Mei-ling cringes at this. Much though she respects her parents, her choice to replace "beautiful – petite/dainty" with "rose - intelligent, skilful" was ideological as much as anything, and impossible to communicate to her parents in a way that also saves face. So her mother continues oblivious: Remember that Ling can also mean 'small bell', and that the 'before dawn/rise high/reach the clouds' connotations of Mei-ling's calligraphic choice some how don't quite match artistically. Or perhaps she could consider the 'features, looks' version of "Mei", or the 'plum blossom' so in keeping with her time of birth. When Rose comes up, wanting her mother's attention, Joyleen (chosen, apparently, because it is close in sound to Mrs Lee's original Chinese first name) pats her on the head like she is a cute toy and returns to the book of names.

Meanwhile Bernie (the name he chose for himself to sound 'Australian', and which he urges me frequently to call him) tries to engage me in manly, business discussions. I have a lot of respect for him – for them both. It cannot be easy leaving a country you love because you fear what is happening in it. Their 'trigger' was the secession of Singapore from Malaysia in '65. They feared a spread of the anti-Chinese fervour from Malaysia that had led to the break. Whilst the Lees were very much Singapore in name, Mei-ling's parents in fact hailed from northern Malaysia, of the Cantonese stock who went across to work the tin mines there a century before. Mr Lee trained to be a lawyer in Melbourne under the Colombo plan, and it was logical that this was the country he would migrate to when he became uncertain about the future on the Malay Peninsula.

Mei-ling seems to think he had some idealistic notion that he could, through legal measures, wield some influence in favour of his relatives back in Malaysia in the face of the anti-Chinese backlash. In reality, what he had learnt was Australian law of British heritage, and he has since in practice turned his back on his origins and embraced the Australian corporate system. These days he assists the Malaysian corporate giants navigating the intricate waters of Australian corporate law and doesn't speak a word to them in any language other than English.

Mei-ling says that her earliest memories are of him admonishing his wife because she spoke to him in Cantonese. "Speak English!" he would say, almost violently. Mei-ling says she can remember his oiled hair shaking with the vehemence of the command. As a child Mei-ling was taken to drive-in movies, fed meat pies, and watched the footy on tv with her Dad. She went to state schools, so that she would learn about equality and fairness and all that it was to be a "good Australian".

Bernie openly applauds Mei-ling's achievements and tells her to "go for it" and "have a good one", for that is the Australian way. But there is always a backhander not far away which asks her about the security of her current position, and he tells her about entrepreneurs who graduated from her year who are now doing so well in Melbourne, and about how good it is that I am doing the MBA, for there will bound to be a good job at the end of it.

It is painful to watch. And it is of course not until Mei-ling points out to me that back in Southern China it is the Chung Yeung ancestor worship festival at the moment that I realise the reasons given by the Lees for their visit – to celebrate Rose's birthday and see Mei-ling's first big promotional event since her return "back home" – might not be all there is to it.

Meanwhile, Rose wants to take Nanna and Poppa out to see the mushrooms up the back, one of which has grown quite splendidly and is actually overshadowing all of the rest, and all both grandparents can do is talk about picking it and cooking it. Rose's face just falls. Neither grandparent can understand why she collapses into tears.

Which is all a source of stress Mei-ling doesn't need right now. We are lucky we do not have sufficient room for them to actually stay in the house. I've known them both almost as long as I've known Mei-ling, but have never spent such a concerted period of time with them. But we've had lovely day today, with a birthday party for Rose on the back veranda. Mei-ling took some time out of rehearsal and came home early with Phillipa. And Jennifer was here, along with Sharon and Helen and their kids, plus a couple of other parents from the Play Group. And Robert and Dale. And of course Mr and Mrs Lee.

Nothing too big. Just a nice little tea party on the back veranda, with jelly and cakes, and some savouries I bought for the adults from a local bakery, and cups of tea, champagne for those that wanted it.

Rose and I have been making little Pucks out of jam tart and mince pie foils lately. It's a bit of a run-up to Christmas thing because they make nice, tinkly decorations; but it's also an attempt to sensitise Rose to the story of the promotion Mei-ling is currently preparing – Puck is the magical character who links it all together, and Rose and I have been making up all sorts of stories about the magic he can do, playing with them up amongst the mushrooms, which Rose now thinks are 'magic' (if only she knew the 70s connotation!). So we have now those hung about the veranda, to clink away in the occasional breeze.

And we have been here a year. So much has changed from this time last year, when we were crammed into the little apartment in Westside, with just Phillipa as a friend and Robert and Dale as new strangers. Now Rose has friends of her own and we have a house of our own and a life here. And Rose is so much more aware. Nothing too formal in terms of games. She was glad just to have the other kids there, to run around the garden, jump on the old mattress in the family room, grapple with the unwieldy concept of "Pass The Parcel" (my one concession to "Birthday Party"). It was a lovely event.

I don't think I have ever been so aware of "a year" with such a sense of achievement and wonder. And it's mostly to do with Rose, and my sense of her growth. I can't believe how much love there is at the centre of my life. Right at its very centre. I sometimes imagine what it is going to be like when she grows up and becomes a teenager and doesn't want to be hugged and kissed. These are such special times.

*

Steps

I took Rose to see *Dream* today. It was wonderful. Rose insisted
we count all of the steps we had to climb in order to reach the
seats right at the back of the circle - the only company seats
available. First there were the steps up to the front door of the
theatre. Then there were the steps from the box office (where we
picked up our tickets) up to the foyer. Then there were the two
gracious, curving sweeps of velvet-carpeted steps that took us up
to the front of the circle. Then there were the narrower, steeper
steps that led us up to the back of the circle. Rose was very
impressed. "So many steps!" she said, making a big deal out of
huffing and puffing and saying "It's alright, Daddy. I can
manage" many times. To us, of course, steps are nothing. But to a
child... and of course it occurred to me she never uses the front
steps to our house, because we always get out of the car in the
driveway and enter by the back door. And in Singapore, we were
still carrying her really.

She enjoyed the production. Mei-ling was supposed to join us but
some drama kept her backstage until the event was over. Rose's
face was just alive in spillage from the lights. She gloried in each
change of set, each new display of colour, music and costume.
While she couldn't have understood much of the language, or the
subtleties of the cross-cultural allegory, she was with the
spectacle and the 'characters' all the way.

Whenever her attention wavered I would ask her what was
happening now. And she always knew. The mummy and daddy
fairies were arguing over their baby. The four friends were lost in
the wood, and fell asleep with the mushrooms. The music was

different now. The dancing was different now. The man had become a donkey and none of his friends knew it was him. They were playing a story and one of them was the wall. She wouldn't like to be the wall. She would rather be the donkey. He was funny. Being up the back, we were free to talk quietly without disturbing anyone overly.

It was a packed auditorium. Saturday matinee, full of families. Apparently the seats are selling really well, even the weeknight performances – talk of extending after Christmas. Which is great, given the appalling press. Mei-ling has been really set up over this. King's only national travel writer, Charlotte Chambers, has obviously been biding her time. And there is more than her behind it.

For a start, she reviewed the show for the Cooksland Herald as well as the National Weekly; unprecedented, but both papers are owned by the Raven Press. And she'd obviously been talking to Chamberlain beforehand. Rabbited on about how outraged she was at the outlandish amount of money lavished on the set, and even that was poorly used by the director. Which was exactly the line Kendall Chamberlain was running in production week.

He was just pissed off because Mei-ling had brought in a lighting designer she used to work with at Surrey Street, and they weren't showing off his work to its 'best aspect'. In reality, Mei-ling was just trying to tone it down because the Performance Centre's workshop (Mei-ling had subcontracted them to leave Kings Company's workshop to concentrate on Malthorpe's promotion) had done such a bad job on the set – cheap materials that wobbled and didn't fit together properly, badly executed scenic artwork. It looked amateurish. Difficult to believe that Max Kingsbury didn't have a hand in that.

She brought Juneen in as contract production/stage manager and started to understand from the inside the problems she had previously. The mechanists and production crew were openly rude on set and couldn't care less whether the show worked or not. Mei-ling would be onstage with Juneen trying to solve a problem and one of the 'mechs' would sound off: "Why doncha talk to us? We're the ones that've got to do it." Whereas if it were a male director and stage manager from a performing arts company, they would have readily accepted the standard protocol: the creative director confers with the stage manager, the stage manager directs the crew. No respect for the level of communication required to think on your feet and solve a problem. Just slovenly, churlish men who aren't getting the level of attention they are used to from women. And, of course and perhaps not coincidentally, they are all employed by Maxwell Kingsbury and the Performance Centre. Right up to opening night Mei-ling had never seen a straight run-through without unnecessary hitches.

Then at the opening itself, apparently Chamberlain stormed up to the Minister for the Arts, Doug Dingwall, right in front of Derek Barrimore and Harold Winterbourne, and openly disparaged Mei-ling's direction. Claimed she knew absolutely nothing about design and had actually worked *against* his set in her direction of the event. Said she wasn't a director's bootlace, and he wasn't the only one who thought so. His trump card insult was that she would be better off working in the performing arts – as if this was somehow inferior!

Of course Mei-ling has had no wind of this. We only heard about the outburst from Derek Barrimore afterwards. I think in the end she was glad to have her parents with her. Introducing them gave her something proactive to do, and took the limelight off. She was shaken by the poor quality of the set, and both angry and anxious on behalf of the talent because they hadn't had a clear run-through, and knew it. The circus performers were particularly nervous.

Anyway, next day Kendall's mate Nimrod Hannah is in Mei-ling's office – she had actually invited him in to offer him a creative slot in next year's program – and he starts trying to lecture Mei-ling about the proper integration of musicians and circus into promotional events. He's the instant expert because he's just back from a community tourism project in Canberra – the sort of thing Mei-ling was doing ten years ago! Having only met the man once, I can just see him preening in his long nosed, pointy chinned way, beaming condescension into Mei-ling's brain.

And of course what else should Charlotte Chambers' review criticise? The lack of integration of circus performers and musicians. And the unnecessary expense of bringing in musicians from interstate when there were perfectly good brass musicians available in King. So who's been talking to whom?

Finally she criticised Mei-ling for "hiding behind the apron strings of some of Australian tourism's finest minds and stand-out performers from the theatre industry before revealing her particular brand of tourism promotion". She sincerely hoped this was not the shape of things to come and called for a serious review of a government funding strategy that saw "this sort of promotion" leading a major transformation of arts funding policy. Isn't it dangerous, Chambers writes, to continue with this strategy in the light of the federal government's warnings on the relationship between cultural tourism and terrorism? When of course the 'cultural' has never come into the Howard Way harangue: just 'tourism'.

So, like Kingsbury (and are we surprised?), she is simply refusing to acknowledge cultural tourism as the leading edge it has become, to the point of 'reviewing' *Dream* as if it were 'theatre'. And of course, within days of her review appearing, there is a crawling letter from Byron Wetherall in the Herald praising Chambers for her "strong and fearless" stance! I'm not into conspiracy theories, but honestly...

And of course Arte De Leon is, funnily enough and definitely quite by coincidence, back in town just in time for the end of Mei-ling's first year of work – just case there happened to be a spare job going?

Thankfully, the consumers are voting with their feet. And subscriptions to Mei-ling's program for next year are already filling fast – both the tours and the promotional events. People do actually like this stuff. It's big, cheap and accessible, thanks to its superior sponsorship potential to the performing arts. The agencies should be pleased. And, apart from Charlotte Chambers, reports in the local press are fairly favourable. A bit mixed, but then most of these writers are just staff journos on suburban weeklies.

And Mei-ling was pleased that Rose liked it. She took us backstage afterwards and introduced Rose to the man who played the donkey, and the man who played the wall, and the woman who played the "mummy fairy". And of course Rose had to go and see the mushrooms from the set. Couldn't quite come to terms with the fact that they were not real. Insisted they were magic nevertheless. And we all counted the steps as we moved from one part of the catacombs that represent the backstage of the Performance Centre to another. And when we got home, we took her up the front steps, so that we could count those too.

*

House Names

Mei-ling and I are thinking of naming the house "Rose Cottage", even though it is a Cookslander rather than a cottage. Neither of us has owned a house before, so we've never even considered giving one a name. But of course many do. And for us, it's a nice way of celebrating our daughter.

We started to think about it because the next stage (so to speak) in the Kingsbury *vs* Kings Company campaign has been about the naming of the Next Stage: who gets to do it, and what the criteria should be. Kingsbury keeps throwing around the names of political patrons like Tresgothic, the Premier, or Dingwall, the Tourism and Arts Minister, and various other ingratiating suggestions. Whereas Mei-ling remains true to her brief, and says the name should be something of commercial value that attracts audiences and helps the public identify the venue with what it celebrates.

She has no idea what such a name might be. Frankly, she doesn't care, and is sick of the dogged pettiness of the politics. Which was why we turned to more pleasant thoughts, such as Rose. It is really lovely to have these Sunday mornings to ourselves. Not that we don't enjoy our times in bed when Rose pays us a morning visit. Mei-ling and Rose play together so well, I love just being there for the fun of it. But now that Phillipa is taking Rose out on Sunday mornings, we just have these few hours in the week in which we can relax and just be together, as we used to.

I don't know what I expected. I guess I thought we would make love, as we did before Rose was born. But remembering back, of course, we never did make love much then either – not in Singapore, anyway. Mei-ling's job was at such a level, she either slept, talked or was preparing for her next project. Working in another culture, she was constantly 'on alert', actively interpreting her world as well as her job every waking second. It was only because we both wanted to have a baby that we made time for it at all. And then we were making a baby, which was an act of love, but the baby was what we both desired of each other.

And since Rose has been in our lives, she has provided an additional focus to work that yields relaxation and relief for Mei-ling. So Mei-ling's energy tends to go into that avenue of release, rather than sex. And interestingly enough, what we actually end up doing on these Sunday mornings is sleep in, make a cup of tea when we wake up, and sit up in bed talking. Often laughing. There is something very therapeutic about a good laugh.

This morning, having started off on the next stage for The Next Stage, we got onto the names of the so-called leadership in the Cooksland tourism industry. I don't know why it has taken us so long to get around to them. I guess when you come into a new 'culture', you try to accept it as you find it, to give yourself the best chance of 'fitting in'. But as we started to talk about them – I think we were back with Nimrod Hannah and his lecture to her the other day about the appropriate use circus performers in cultural tourism events. He's such a queen, Mei-ling was saying. Yes, a preening queen, I rejoined. And who calls their kid Nimrod anyway? Perhaps that was part of his problem. Probably a couple of hippies, we conjectured, who were into Greek mythology. Anachronistically, because all of the other hippies were into Buddhist legends and Taoist symbolism and Hindu myths. So they were always protective of little Nimrod because they secretly knew they'd given him a name that stood out from all of the other kids in hippy high school – like Zen, and Siva, and Siddhartha, and Rama, and Parvati, and Sita. And were always telling him it was okay to be gay by way of compensation, just in case he was. And so of course he came to be.

And what about Arte de Leon? Surely he made that up himself? His real name has to be Dick Pratfall, and he got kicked around at school so much he determined to show them all when he grew up. But of course he was a repressed gay because a bunch of really nasty boys gang-banged him one night on the way home from school, so he retreated into aestheticism and was never able to properly 'come out'. Just ponce around a lot, reinvent himself as a tour impresario, and drop out of commitments at the last minute because the rape had given him a performance complex and he was secretly afraid he couldn't really do it, whatever 'it' was.

And what pair of ill-meaning parents named their little Wetherall 'Byron'? English lecturers from university who spent entire weekends reading Victorian poetry to each other, boring poor little Byron to death. No wonder he ran away to sea, and devoted himself to finding devious ways of bringing about the epic downfall of others.

Then there was Lillith Plant: surely even Lillium or Lily would have been kinder – at least then her name would have been a genuine laugh. But Lillith? Even those who called their kids biblical names usually chose somewhat more familiar epithets like Ruth or Naomi.

Then we got on to the interstaters. Tristan Malthorpe, for instance. The surname was miserable enough in itself, but to add Tristan to it was to mount sin upon sin. Apparently this is a character in an opera by Wagner, so the intellectual world inhabited by his parents must have been laden with doom and dread from wall to wall.

Then there is Ranald Whippet – a man with a tiny but virulent dick who just has to get it in, but does it so quickly you hardly knew he'd been up you. Again, driven to it as a method of revenge as a kid when everybody picked on him because of his given name. Only to discover years later that it was a spelling mistake by a dyslexic clerk at Births, Deaths and Marriages – it took years of lawsuits from disgruntled parents to bring the NSW State Government to the realisation that they had a minor but significant moron in their ranks. Ranald really should have been a Ronald. But by then it was too late. He had used it in public and there was no going back. And anyway, he thought it gave him a certain air of *je ne sais quoi*. Which, if he had bothered actually studying French at school, he would have known meant an ontological air of ignorance.

Anyway, by this time the tears were just running down our faces. What is it about the tourism industry that attracts such nominative misfits? And then we were quiet for a bit, staring at our still incomplete wardrobe. And then Mei-ling wondered whether anyone said the same sort of thing about us for naming our daughter Rose. But too many people express such genuine delight when they hear her name, so glad to see it coming back into the lexography, I said I shouldn't think so. Although among the malcontents of King's tourism community, we were sure any miserly jibe was fair game.

And then we talked about naming the house after her. And before we knew it, there she was, coming back in through the porch doors, Phillipa behind her, enthusing over the milkshake she had at the coffee shop Phillipa had taken her to with Jennifer. It was too hot for swimming, Phillipa said. And there seemed a perverse logic to that too.

Rose will miss Phillipa over Christmas. As usual, Phillipa doesn't hang around for the celebration, or the family time. Stuffs herself into a back pack and takes herself away into the bush, remerges ten days later a new woman, she says. Going to Tasmania this year, to *do* the Cradle Mountain to Lake St Clair walk. What, I say with mock horror, not with *people*, in a *party*??? No, she says, she's not going that way. Which is, evidently, a Tasmanian joke. (A Tasmanian tells a mate he's driving a flock of sheep to Melbourne. "So how're you gonna get 'em across Bass Strait?" the mate asks. "Nah," says Tassie, "We're not goin' that way.")

*

Toilet

Rose has mastered the toilet. Isn't it strange how such small and modest achievements take on such huge proportions during parenthood? The first time she grasps Mei-ling's scarf on our first trip back to Australia with her, lying on her back looking up into Mei-ling's laughing eyes at Melbourne airport, waiting for our luggage to appear on the carousel in the arrivals hall. The first time she tries to stand, and falls down immediately, but doesn't cry. Is just bemused, and tries again. The first time she starts to crawl. Suddenly an arrival home takes on new meaning, because she understands the distance between her and the person entering the room. It is no longer just a smaller version of a face she knows appearing suddenly in her world. It is the same face, a distance away. And it gets bigger as she crawls towards it.

She has been using the potty most of the time we've been back, but it's always been a hit-and-miss affair. I've just got used to bucketing poos and wees down the toilet. But gradually, without us even noticing, she has become more and more accurate with her timing. I have now started leaving the side of her cot down because she gets up herself to come and tell me she needs to go. She no longer needs those all-night diaper-type pants. And today I found her actually sitting on the toilet, all by herself. Just pushed the door ajar and there she was, chatting away to herself. I tried not to make too much of it. Just told her she looked comfortable.

And she smiled and agreed. She was obviously quietly pleased with herself.

I am wondering whether it was because we took her to visit her new kindergarten yesterday. And she saw the child-sized toilets they have there, and figured that was what she was going to have to use from now on. It was great watching her get to know this entirely new, Rose-sized environment. She has been used to play group in the church hall, but that sort of comes and then goes. We arrive, equipment comes out, Rose and Bronwyn and Sharelle play, time comes to leave and we pack up and there is just the same old bare-floored shellac-smelling box of a hall again. But the East King Kindergarten is a whole new proposition. The chairs are her size. The tables are her size. There are shelves and curtained cupboards all at her height, with plastic trays she can pull out, each with a different activity inside. There are books at her height. Even the two teachers sit on chairs that are almost at her height. And then there are the child-sized toilets and washbasins.

It seems odd to me to see toilets in the same room as the classroom – of course it needs to be a washable area, but is separated only by a low partition rather than a floor-to-ceiling wall. Because to the kids it doesn't matter. Bodily functions aren't something they are embarrassed about yet. Kids can wander through while others are dispensing with their natural waste and neither gives a second thought. Whereas it is important that the teacher can see them, just in case they get caught short or need help wiping their bottoms or pulling up their knickers or turning on the tap. There is such a lovely, unabashed logic to it.

Narelle and Malcolm were in fact a little worried that Rose isn't fully toilet trained. They said they were sure she'd be fine, but normally they don't accept pupils until they can manage the toilet by themselves. And suddenly, a day later, here she is, on her own throne!

I think it's coming as a bit of a shock to Mei-ling: that Rose is virtually starting school already. It will only be for two days a week – two mornings for the first term. But even so, I think she thought there would be something of Rose's childhood for her. That she would get some of the time there was to play with her little girl. But already she can see that gap closing as the two cliffs come together to clap Rose's entry into institutional education. But Rose is clearly ready for this next step. The play group has shown that.

As for me, I'm looking forward to a time when I no longer empty the potty slops. Something you take for granted, and think will never end. And I kind of hang around hoping we're doing this well. I can remember the act of trying to keep my toilet in when I was a kid, and still like my privacy in the loo. Rose must be learning that: observing what I do (close the door) as distinct from what she does. Luckily Mei-ling doesn't care, and offers an alternative 'open door loo policy'.

And as long as we continue to reinforce her good practices, hopefully she will just develop her own positive self-image and her bodily processes will flow beautifully, regardless of the architectural constraints of the boxes in which we hide our ablutions. I'm sure men invented toilets, to contain the explosiveness of their lifelong attempt at self-control. Or perhaps women invented them, to contain the explosiveness of their men.

*

124

Window Frame

I used to spend hours looking out of windows when I was a kid. Allowing my eyes to roam a real world beyond the glass where something active and alive was either happening or inevitable. As if what occurred inside the house was what we did while waiting to go outside. I can always remember my parents kicking us out of the house when we got too much as kids. "For goodness sakes go outside, will you?" As if outside was where we kids "did" things. "If you want to play, play outside." "If you want to build that, do it outside." "If you're going to make that racket, make it outside." Only smaller duties happen inside, like preparing meals, cleaning clothes and mending or making them, and they only prepare you for going out. Although the man's home is supposed to be his castle, in reality his realm is beyond its walls.

But now I am an adult and a parent, I don't have time to sit and look out of them, windows. They are pictures I glance up, down or across at in passing, while I am doing something else. I notice the frame as much as I do the window, because it is the rectangular rim of the lens that snaps and snaps again the many facets of my ongoing understanding of what is "outside".

I live my time inside the house with a continuing sense of what is happening outside, and yet that continuum is really a set of pictures framed from many angles and planes. Raining one minute. Sunny the next. Part of a car in one frame. Another part of it in another. Gone in the next. Gates across the road left open. Then closed. Traces of movement left in the frame.

But tonight, the frame looks totally inward. For I have adorned it – well, one of them – with Christmas lights, and placed on a small table beneath it our traditional sprig of Christmas Bush in Mei-ling's favourite weighty stone vase. And before that are now our Christmas presents, wrapped up and arranged in mild disarray, as

125

if hastily assembled there by a busy Father Christmas. Mei-ling and I have been working on them most of the night, after a bit of a falling out when she arrived home – which was late. Her last appointment for the day had stretched on forever. I was really annoyed because it was Christmas Eve, and I wanted Mei-ling to be home to share it with Rose. And me.

Rose has a real sense of what's happening this year. Last year it was still a surprise – to wake up and find presents at the foot of your bed, in a stocking. Even though we did the Father and Mother Christmas bit, she only really understood the presents. But this year I have read and played her Raymond Briggs' *The Snowman* and *Father Christmas*, and we've got a couple of Christmassy cartoons out from the rental outlet, and she's noticed the decorations and colours coming into the shops.

So today we bought some lights, and I arranged them around the window frame in the lounge nearest her bedroom, and I found some Christmas Bush at a florist down in South King; so we put that in Mei-ling's favourite vase, which we then decorated with a ribbon round the vase and tinsel around the bush, especially for mummy. So I just wanted Mei-ling to be home to see what we had done.

But six o'clock came and went, and I rang Mei-ling but she sounded tense and terse and said she was in a meeting. So I didn't want to bother her again and it started to get dark and Rose was getting tired and, in the end, after we had turned the lights on around the window frame and they had started to blink, I put Rose to bed. Talked to her about Mother Christmas driving Father Christmas in the sleigh as far as the equator, then changing the deer for kangaroos. They would be on their way right now. Sang her some carols – those that I could remember. Hummed those I couldn't.

And by then I was really angry, because it was too late to pick Mei-ling up, and I had no idea if there was anyone there to give her a lift home. I worry about the idea of her leaving the Cultural Centre alone at night. All those concrete walkways, poorly lit and deserted after the art gallery and museum have closed and the staff gone home. Great place for druggies to lurk and shoot up and mug Mei-ling. My imagination runs on an unnecessary film loop.

So I set about preparing a sausage meat stuffing for the turkey I had insisted on buying, even though it is far too big for the three of us. So angry with myself about that too, and about spending money on food and wrapping paper and decorations we can't really afford. Although of course we can really: I am just punishing myself, just to make sure I really appreciate the joy of Christmas when we finally get to it.

Because deep down I miss the Christmases of my youth and want to impart some of that joy and pleasure to Rose and Mei-ling, but feel inadequate and incapable and not a provider and so do my humble bit and you know how the merry male story goes. Love me. Nurture me. Look how loving and caring I am. Here I am stuffing this stupid turkey in the hope it will bring some hope into our lives – well it's bound to, isn't it, with all of the tension and imperative I will force into preparing and cooking it throughout the day!

And of course there is always an undercurrent, isn't there. Yes, I am ultra-tense because I set myself the target of finishing the honours thesis by the end of the year, and here we are at December 24th and I've run up umpteen hours of Jennifer and still haven't finished. And the political backlash against cultural tourism is firming up, so Mei-ling's loss-leading strategy could be under threat, so I might have to get into the workforce sooner, mightn't I. And now here Mei-ling is, late home. Goodness, the astounding fatalism of it all. Ho, ho, ho!

Anyway, eventually she rings to say she has finished, and Phillipa (bless her) is still there and will give her a lift home. Which Phillipa does, and shares our Macaroni Cheese, and a glass of wine. And in a way, it's good that Phillipa is there. Someone to diffuse the situation. Talk to both of us while I metaphysically "turn my back" on the situation by preparing and serving the meal. Which Mei-ling doesn't want to eat. She is wrung out because she has spent three hours with Lillith Plant, who has been holding out on signing two contracts with the company for major roles in activity for next year Mei-ling has already announced in her publicity.

During the first hour Plant harangues Mei-ling with the professional outrage of the offer. Why wasn't she offered a full promotion in the next year? It is professionally embarrassing. People will take it as a comment on her promotion this year. Everyone in the industry knows why *The Rural Ward* failed, and it *wasn't* down to her! Mei-ling reassures her there is no slight intended: there just isn't a slot for her. *The Rural Ward* was very well received locally despite the difficulties, which nobody outside the company noticed. Exactly Ms Plant's point. King's Company is inconsistent, and does nothing to develop local professionals. Mei-ling points out that she has had two major contracts with the company during the year, represented the company at the National Tourism Workshop, and directed a major promotion for them. Now she is being offered two major roles in next year's program. But how can any professional live on that? Plant cries, even though she has her own business, and so it goes on.

Then in the next hour all of the aggression and bravado dissolves into self-pity and tears, and Ms Plant ends up telling Mei-ling how hard it is for women in the profession in King, the glass ceiling above franchise management, and how she in particular has suffered with marriage break-ups and illness and the ongoing indifference of the state tourism commission. And Mei-ling finds herself increasingly thrust into a counselling role she is untrained to handle. But handle it she does, refuses to take on any of the transferences or projections and, in the end, asks Plant to sign the contracts. Which she does.

So by the time I have understood all of this, I have mellowed, and am angry with myself for, as usual, prejudging Mei-ling and not exercising better control over my own thoughts. And in the end Phillipa goes (home to pack – she is off tomorrow). And Mei-ling apologises for being late. And I lie and say I was worried for her. But am still angry with myself. Even more so when Mei-ling finally dissolves into tears, because the whole time she was there dealing with the psychological dysfunctions of this overgrown child, all she wanted to do was get home and spend Christmas Eve with Rose and I. And that made me cry too. I don't think they pay this woman enough for doing what she does.

Anyway, we had a bit of a cuddle, and then got out the presents that had been sent by various parents, aunts and uncles, and the stuff I have been buying for Rose. And we wrapped presents and drank wine and arranged them under the tree. Rose's stocking was last. We both snuck in together and placed that carefully on the end of her bed. And went to bed ourselves and made love. Her Christmas present, she said, because she hasn't been able to get away to buy me anything. I told her to forget the Christmas present. It was just us making love – something we don't do enough these days.

And now Mei-ling is sleeping soundly. And I have got up to place her Christmas present under the "tree", because I didn't have the chance before we went to bed. And I look at her in slumber and hope to whatever there is to hope to that she gets some rest over this next fortnight or so. But in the meantime, of course, have been reminded of a quote by the post-structuralist and feminist sociologist, Rhea Barnett, which I just had to find, and have spent the last half an hour doing so:

For all the structure and system in the world, if it is populated with weakness of mind the action of culture will reduce it to that bottom line of personality, ego.

Seems to sum up King's sum of cultural expertise, doesn't it.

*

Overhead Fans

I have finally discovered the value of the famous Cookslander cross. The last few days have been so hot and humid, I have just had front and back door open, and the windows in the kitchen and the lounge, and lain on the floor at the centre of the "cross" trying to make the most of whatever movement of air there is, however faint. And I have been out and bought overhead fans for the bedroom, study and Rose's room and hired an electrician to come and install. He arrives tomorrow, and it won't be a moment too soon. These weatherboard houses are like paper. The heat just walks through the walls and marches about the house as it pleases. We hang out for the Easterly that comes in from the sea at around four, and crawl out onto the front veranda to bask in the cool change.

Never mind. It forced Mei-ling to relax in the few days since New Year. Good thing too, as no sooner is she back at work than she if off to Melbourne to view a cross-cultural tourism promotion of the Melbourne Tourism Commission's she has bought for the coming Cooksland year sight-unseen. The new production manager Phillipa found in Perth is accompanying her to view the set. Good to see the company at full strength again. The production manager role in King's Company is vital in bridging performing arts and tourism.

I had a funny evening with Phillipa tonight. Quite spooky. She came round socially because she said she was lonely and we never got to talk just to each other anymore. I thought that was fair enough. She is my friend too, after all.

Anyway, it turns out she is "man-lonely". It's this "lost father" and "lost mother" syndrome of hers'. Can't bear to be without a love interest as a surrogate father, but as soon as she has one is so fearful of losing them through some fault she is unaware of, she repulses them herself. That's the psychology of it, anyway.

I tell her how much we appreciate the Sunday mornings she gives us, and how much Rose enjoys the swim. Or the trip to the park, or the coffee shop.

But the conversation is going somewhere else. I get the strong impression that she is talking about me, sounding me out as the love interest. It is one of those conversations full of sighs and unexplicated statements like: Oh don't you wish it was simple sometimes? Don't you wish you could just make the approach and have done with it? Friendship can be such a stumbling block, can't it? You don't want to lose it but if you want to get beyond that… Have you ever been in that situation where you really want to become intimate with someone but there is another relationship in the way that you don't want to risk? And: Oh god, two weeks in the bush on my own – I need a fuck!

All very un-Phillipa. She's usually very private about her love life. With me, anyway. Besides, she has usually been in relationships with friends of mine in the past. I've never seriously thought about having sex with her myself. But once all of these left-unsaids started to roll out, my own sweating ego willingly

131

comes up smiling and says: hallo? Someone interested in me? Yes, I could walk through those mood swing saloon doors and be loved, made love to. Yup. I can be that man.

I should've known better, of course. If Phillipa were going to proposition me she'd be far more direct. But after the meal she was lounging around with such languor and longing, it was hard not to enter into the web of innuendo and I-think-you-know-what-I-mean. I felt so embarrassed when she got up to go with a sigh, told herself she would work things out, and thanked me for allowing her to unburden herself. It can be difficult sometimes, and when her other friends are intimately involved. But it was good to "catch up".

I never did find out who the lover/potential lover is, or who the other characters in the intrigue are, but am thankful that I didn't step into the fan. Ever the faithful adviser. Ah these male roles… so easy. Cool ego down. Tuck back in box. Hope he's grown up a little more next time.

*

Swimming Pool

Rose had her first swimming lesson today. The state government offers them free of charge. There are so many pools in individual homes, back-yard drowning is a real safety issue. Plus Cooksland has the climate for those early morning training sessions that produce Olympic champions.

I always remember so vividly the impact of flying into Australia from Singapore on Mei-ling's company-funded annual return trips. Didn't matter which capital city we flew into, it was always as dawn broke, and the ground was studded with the little gold medallions of property dam. And I always had the same thought: if only they could combine all of that water, instead of each owner having their own private collection, each one massively subject to evaporation, wouldn't they all be better off?

And then, as the sun rose and we descended over the city, so the pale blue jewels would start to appear amidst the red and green rooves, like cloisonné, but suburbs and suburbs of it. One backyard pool for every cluster of three or four houses. Broken by the occasional rectangle of public baths. It was just so 'coming home' for me.

Anyway, most of the playgroup have enrolled in Swimsafe, so it was a sort of outing for us all. Standing around under the various metal shades, still feeling hot and bothered but at least able to chat while someone else teaches our children.

And of course all of that sunscreen. Handfuls of white glub rubbed in every conceivable square millimetre of exposed skin. Sunsmart all-in-one suits. We are such a cancer-conscious country these days. Gone are the bronzed torsos of old.

What amazed me was Rose herself. I was so surprised to see a side of her character I didn't know. It wasn't just that all of the other kids dutifully got into the pool once instructed, whereas Rose didn't. It was that, as the instructor persisted in telling her to get in, she retreated – right back to the wall of the changing room block. Folded her arms.

This is the point at which I leave things with Rose. Never force her to do anything she doesn't really want to. Support well-motivated risk-taking, praise adventure and achievement, but don't place failure to take risks in the negative context of a win-lose conflict. Just non-reinforce it and look for the positives. It's not as if she hasn't been in the pool before, either with Mei-ling and I, or with Phillipa. So no-one understands what the problem is now. Best to leave it to Rose herself to work out.

But Josie, the instructor, kept going: Come on Rose, everyone else has got in. You don't want us to start without you, do you? Everybody else is having a good time. I'll count to three – one – two – And just as she said "three" Rose bolted forward from the changing room wall with determination and purpose and climbed down the steps into the pool, and joined her friends. "Well done, Rose. Good to have you with us. Now then everyone, listening to me. I want you to…."

It was like seeing someone I hadn't known before. An independent personality. And certainly one (two, three) to remember for the future!

*

Rose and Hooks

I had sex with a man today. Phillipa had offered to take Rose out for a swim. Said she feels she has been neglecting us over Christmas, as she went off on her usual annual bush bash – down in Tasmania this time. I assured her it didn't matter – we had a nice time together as a family. But she is still taking a bit of time out of work, so I thanked her for the offer.

I thought I would automatically take the time out to work on my thesis, but instead I invited Robert C over to help me finish the picture hanging. There were still the smaller prints and watercolours that would look silly hanging on ruddy great brass chains. I'd bought some of those cheap plastic four-pin bang-in-the-wall hooks. I haven't seen him since just before Christmas and thought it would be nice to catch up.

While we were hammering and positioning, after general talk about how we were respectively going, and how Christmas had been etc., he asked me if I'd thought any more about my sexuality in relation to my choice of role reversal. I'd been talking about always being the one to cook Christmas dinner in our relationship, because I was the one who always felt the need to 'make' Christmas.

Even as I told him I hadn't, I knew that I had. Been thinking about it somewhere in my mind, but certainly a part of it I hadn't been aware of consciously. And even as I became aware of it, I was also became conscious of Robert sexually. As in, a certain tension. Not aversion, but excitement, of the possibility. I dismissed it, of course. But still coveted that certain thrill.

Anyway, Robert didn't seem to notice. Went on to say that he wasn't sure how much longer he would last with Dale. Working together on the Diversity Project isn't working, so to speak. He said it was fine being together on the Tourism Australia Council (which is how they met), and it was fine being together in public as Dale's partner. But the complexities of working together in contrasting but interdependent roles on a project brought out all manner of differences that served only to amplify those in the relationship that already frustrated him. Like sleeping with the window open. He was joking, but he confessed that such minor resentments just made him feel worse about himself, and Dale.

I empathised. Said I found exactly the same effect in my relationship with Mei-ling (the petty resentments), and it was good to know somebody else shared the experience. He asked me how Mei-ling and I met, and how we were going. I confessed we did not make love much these days, because of stresses of the job,

I guessed, and for me the stresses of taking on a new role, of primary care giver. And, frankly, a certain sense of insecurity about my personal future as a professional, a man with a career.

This was a common theme for Robert and I, and we joked and chatted about it easily. I found myself watching for his smile, so easy and boyish, affable. A real grin to it. And that excitement started to return. An anticipation that caught my breath. Anyway, after we'd finished the job he said he was hot, and had walked through the heat to get here in the first place. Could he take a shower? I said yes as if it were normal, not wishing to offend. I gave him a fresh towel and made us a cup of tea. But during his absence, I found myself listening for the shower. Listening for him. With that same sense of anticipation. I hadn't felt like this before. Not with a man. I liked it, but it made me nervous.

Not long after I heard the shower cease, he called me in. He wanted me to look at a mole on his back. He was worried in case it might be cancer. So corny in retrospect. But I'm a believer. I went in, and of course he was naked. I looked at the mole, trying not to look at his body, and said it didn't look cancerous to me, but then I wouldn't really know. He said he hoped he didn't make me feel uncomfortable. I said of course not. He said that, not being a 'sporting type', he had never had the chance to get used to being naked with males when he was younger. Even though it was something he had wanted.

I empathised again. I was used to being in a sports changing room naked with males. But was always self-conscious about revealing myself – tried to be the last one in the shower, along with the other smaller, skinnier, less athletic boys. Whereas the successful athletes – the 'in crowd' – were always uninhibited, making jokes about their nakedness, comparing the size of their dicks, flicking each other with towels.

As I was talking, I was remembering as I spoke a sports teacher we had then, who was about as un-athletic as you could get. Short. Tubby. A smoker. But loved to hang around the change rooms, supposedly being 'in' with the boys as a coach, joking, giving them cigarettes on the quiet, but always picking on this one kid. A big kid, but not a fat kid. However definitely a middle class kid, whose dad was also a teacher, and a lay preacher. The sort of kid who had big lips and slightly girlish eyes, and who the 'in group' always found it easy to ridicule and bully because he wanted to be one of them but was genuinely too nice to actually achieve in-group snideness.

One time the sports teacher – Taffy, we used to call him – got stuck into Martin, was telling him to get in the shower. After a game. Martin was trying to say that he was not showering today, very politely, because he had a bandage on his wrist from a sprain. But Taffy caught him just as he was changing, swirled the towel into a tight whip and was flicking him with it. It was quite violent. But I remember looking at Martin's round bottom wobbling as Taffy flicked it with the towel. And the size of his dick flaccid and wiggling as Taffy drove him towards the showers with the towel. I have never thought about the image since, but I found it deep within me at that moment.

Robert was looking at me in the mirror. He asked me if I had ever kissed a man. I said no. Suddenly I was more nervous than excited. I could have turned away and left, but I didn't. I watched him turn and take my cheek with one hand, and look me in the eye. I don't want you to do something you don't want to, he said. I could have resisted. I could have said no. Maybe it was just because I was a nice guy and did not want to offend. But it was me that moved my mouth towards his, my lips that engaged with his.

It was odd, exchanging tongues with a man. But it was also arousing. I entered an embrace. I ran my hand down his back. I started to feel his buttocks. And could feel, through my jeans, his penis rising, and my own.

He said, with a half-bashful smile, that he felt a little alone (in his nakedness), and did I mind? He was lifting my t-shirt. I let him remove it. Reassuring me it was okay. That I was beautiful. I was breathless as he went to undo my jeans. I was aware of my own erection falling away from my underpants as he eased them down. He asked was there somewhere we could go.

I didn't want to use the bedroom. I knew it wasn't right. I knew this wasn't right. I was betraying Mei-ling. Being 'unfaithful'. But because it was a man, it did not seem 'unfaithful'. I couldn't think straight (sic), I confess. I was very excited. I pulled out the sofa bed. I couldn't stop kissing and caressing him. I just loved the freedom of it. Loved feeling his erect penis against mine. I really wanted to take his into my mouth, and loved the feeling of his mouth around mine at the same time. It was just so erotic. So mutual.

He asked me if I wanted to feel him inside me. I had to say I didn't. I'm far too anally retentive to imagine anything actually going in that way except a doctor's finger in surgical gloves. But he said he wanted to feel me inside him. I said I didn't have a condom, but he said it would be okay; this was my first time, wasn't it? As in, no risk of AIDS.

He got me to rub some baby oil I'd forgotten we had into his anus. I found his buttocks so arousing. And his anus. I couldn't believe how hard my erection was as I applied the oil to it. I always thought of myself as such a soft cock with women.

I can hardly remember being on his back, and inside him. My head was just swimming. It felt so good to be inside a man. Such a release. I seemed to just cum and cum. I was still shaking afterwards. But with the release of it, not with the fear or anxiety.

He stroked me, and said it was okay. We kissed some more, then lay on our backs for a while, staring up at the ornamental plaster rose on the ceiling around the main light in our lounge. He wondered whether it was original, or a reproduction. He reminded me that the lounge had been created out of two rooms and a hallway. But the fact that this rose remained in what would have been the original front room indicated it was probably authentic federation. Then he commented idly that rose-petalling was what they called the act of tonguing a lover's anus in some gay quarters. Mostly the older guys. Then he said I had better shower and he had better go. He was sure I wouldn't want my own Rose to find me in my current circumstances.

By the time I had showered, he was dressed and ready to go. He kissed me again, and said he wasn't sure where this went yet. He really liked me, but he wasn't really sure until today whether I liked him. But he wouldn't want Dale to know. Not just yet. I reckon, I replied, laughing with relief. Me neither. Mei-ling, I mean. It simply hadn't occurred to me that there would be an 'after', or a 'next time'. I had just been there, in the moment.

I don't know what to make of this now. I've tucked it away. Folded it back into the place I opened within myself today. Welcomed Rose back, thanked Phillipa with a hug and a kiss on the cheek, went to pick up Mei-ling, cooked tea and debriefed with her as usual. Went to bed. Told her I loved her. And I do. Nothing has changed. Except that I've had sex with a man. Perhaps it is just that. A one off. A learning experience I can just keep to myself. And perhaps visit from time to time. But I know that's not true. I can't stop thinking about Robert, and being naked with him. I have found someone new inside me.

Garden Path

I keep looking out of the windows at the front of the house, at the twin strips of concrete that climb up from the roadway along the side of the house and disappear under the wheels of our parked car, or at the slab or two of crazy paving that mark the front garden between the pedestrian pavement and our front steps. It has become an obsession. Every second glance is in these two directions. Hoping to see Robert Cunningham's head arriving.

I yearn for him every waking moment I am alone. When I am with Mei-ling, she has my undivided attention. The same with Rose. But when Rose is asleep, and I am left to my own thoughts, it is Robert I find in them. I do not want to presume to ring him. I do not want to admit to myself that I want him to be wanting me. Tell myself he is not really interested in me. Gay guys do this sort of thing all the time, don't they. I am not gay, I tell myself. This is just a new experience. It is the excitement of it, the novelty.

And part of this is true. I know I love Mei-ling. And have always focussed solely on sexual relations with women. Found women desirable. I have never so much as looked at a man in that way. Except, obviously, for Martin Hasluck when he was whipped on the bottom by some repressed bastard of a sports teacher in my UK youth. And yes, my own actions now betray me. My head turns as if in reflex. And the front garden paths are the constant object of my anticipation, and a male lover the content I hope they will yield.

I feel so guilty about this. I have let Mei-ling down. This is something I can never reveal to her. It is a mistake I so want to put behind me. Yet I also want to pick up the phone every five minutes and call Robert. I construct conversations in my head I will have with him, anticipate how these will run. Then scold myself for being so childish. And go around the same block again.

Fundamentally, I like Robert, and am glad to have found a man I can actually talk to beyond the boundaries of patriarchal thought. With whom I can enjoy being with Rose. But I can't just 'call' him now as if nothing has happened. I don't want to place him in a position of obligation, as one who has 'initiated' something I now 'need'. That would be unfair on him. And unfair on me. To be the one vulnerable, when I need to be the one strong for Mei-ling, and for Rose.

In addition, I would not want to get Dale instead. Before, that wouldn't have mattered. Now, because I am a hopeless dissembler, I imagine he would guess just from the tone of my voice. Obviously because these gay guys are just so *sensitive* and *perceptive*, unlike we *straights*. And so off down the garden path again.

But what if …. Just what if….

It's driving me insane. Thank god for Rose. And for a thesis I really MUST finish. Just one more glance at the garden path, in case….

*

Holiday

It's been nice having a quiet 48 hours away from the house, and the city. Even nicer that it's on the company. Reminds me of our holidays from Singapore.

Singapore was always so small, you really had to leave it to take a break. I miss those jaunts now up into Malaysia, or Thailand, or across to the Philippines, or India. So many different versions of the resort, with just enough local cultural flavouring to make it seem authentic. We didn't just stretch out physically; it was an entire, whole-of-being relaxation. I remember reading Senge on the beach at Pangkor – I was just sort of soaking it in, like the coconut oil. And Mei-ling and I making long and languorous love in the afternoon, followed by gin and tonics on the veranda before dinner.

All pre-Rose, of course. And now this unexpected dip back into it. Thanks to Phillipa, although unwittingly in the first instance. Having herself returned from a robust bushwalking holiday, she announced that King's Company needed to comply with a new government requirement for formalised strategic and business plans, to be submitted 'by yesterday'. She was all for locking the entire executive into the Board Room until the gruelling task was accomplished. It was Mei-ling who suggested they come up here to the George's Bay Resort instead. But it was Phillipa who suggested, once we got here, that we stay on for a couple of days extra as a family.

It's been fun dipping into the various pools here. Rose swims to me easily from the edge now, a good ten strokes out. We even took a little dip in the sea. And now with the three of us together, Rose has been swimming easily between the Mei-ling and I, in fairly deep water. No fear. Lots of puff. Although she gets short of breath easily, compared to the other kids at SwimSafe.

And with Mei-ling keen to play with Rose in the pool, and in the adventure playground they have here in the dunes, I have been free to take a few long, deep strokes myself underwater, enjoying that fabulous silence, the light playing around my head in dancing shafts and triangles. Even though we are in the near-tropics, the water is never as warm as it was in South East Asia. But my body still lengthens through it with ease. And I think of Robert Cunningham. And am alone in my guilt. Still want to call him. Still I can't risk seeming forward, can't risk getting Dale instead. Robert, hiding behind the clandestine like a bureaucrat between regulations.

*

I don't know whether it's by association, or whether this is a real issue, but something that has caught in my mind as a result of the company's sessions has been Phillipa's admission to the entire management team that she sees herself as working for the government, not for the company.

It was me who suggested that they go through some of the more organisational culture aspects of corporate planning. It doesn't bother me that I wasn't, as a result, invited to facilitate the session, as I assumed Phillipa would do that, and admirably. So I've only learnt what transpired second hand.

Alicia Driffield's response sounds as I would expect from someone with a corporate background. Vision. Mission. Corporate goals. Tynan McAvaddy, the new production manager, likewise gave an unsurprisingly ill-informed but pragmatic promotion/arts/shopping centre events construction perspective – what does it matter what the vision is? How are we going to build it, where, and how much is it going to cost? But I would've expected a more managerial approach from Phillipa. The fact that she identifies more with bureaucracy is understandable given her time working in it, but she should have left behind the actual government bureaucracy she had been working for before Kings Company.

In their vision and mission exercise she apparently stated quite clearly that, because King's Company was funded largely by the state government, she saw the state as her employer. And as such, she saw herself as beholden to state government policies. Surely, I say to Mei-ling, she understands that the company's corporate plan is for economic independence within three years. Whilst it depends on government subsidy now, the whole thrust of a King's Company business strategy has to be to use sponsorship to act as a profit buffer while the business achieves financial sustainability. Government subsidy simply has to disappear.

Mei-ling does not see Phillipa's admission as the problem I do. She says it's useful that Phillipa has declared her hand so openly. It is also useful that they have a firm link into the Cooksland tourism bureaucracy – it's a channel of communication that can work both ways. Particularly as the government starts to deal with what is shaping up to be a cultural tourism backlash from rural Cooksland, with communities now directly contacting their offices with concerns about the terrorism threat adumbrated by Howard Way last year.

It's such a joke that what was so obviously a political gaff has been translated now into public concern and a 'policy review'! But a joke that seems happily distant from Mei-ling, Rose and I, swimming between each other in the lazy afternoon of an almost-tropical resort towards the north of a vast continent somewhere south of the equator.

*

My Father's House

A copy of my father's will finally arrived today. Barry has been right all along. He didn't amend it after my mother's death. Everything was still left to her. So typical. Didn't want to face the reality. Wanted to maintain things as if she were still alive.

I can't be bothered fighting over it anymore. Too far away. And Barry has probably buried the money anyway, in 'secure investments' from which it will be impossible to 'extract the principal'. If ever I need anything, I just have to ask and he will 'initiate proceedings'. He is just so like Dad, my father's Number One Son: mean-spirited, small minded, insular, xenophobic to the point of racism. I never understood how I came to be so different from him. From them both.

Because I was more like Mum, I guess. I can still remember standing on the platform bidding my father farewell. He stood there in the bitterly cold wind, his eyes watery, whether with sadness or the wind I could not tell, but obdurately uncomprehending in all of their pale blue. He simply could not understand why I was going. Let alone to India. Why I wasn't getting a job and settling down like my older brother.

And I felt such pain, because I wanted him to love me, like he loved everyone else. Well, women. He always loved to cuddle women, and kiss them, albeit playfully. Such a contradiction. All of my girlfriends. Barry's girlfriends. Mum's friends. And so affectionate with Mum. But nothing for us, his sons. Just distance.

I can remember him coming into the bathroom once, while I was in the bath. He had no shame. Sat on the toilet to evacuate his bowels – I could hear them plopping away behind my head. Then flushing, and standing at the sink beside the bath to wash his hands, his pants still down, his long scrotum and flaccid buttocks bare. And he asked me awkwardly if anyone had talked to me at school about the facts of life. I would have been about fourteen, but in my mind I am much smaller, much younger. And I said Yes Dad, they do it when you're twelve these days. And again when you get to fifteen. Big sessions. Male teacher. All the details. Nothing missed. That was about as intimate as we ever got.

I think he was always fearful I would turn out queer. Because I was the 'softy' of his two sons. He was derogatory about 'nancies' in front of me in a way that he never was with Barry. Told me to stand up for myself more, not to give in so much, how important it was to 'be a man', to watch out for 'queers' and 'poofs' – they were all poofs in India, you know - to think about a practical trade instead of this 'writing business'. Even then I was telling him it wasn't writing, it was journalism. And I was going to India to write travel stories.

Who for, he demanded. Did I have a contract? I was just working in a printing firm. (Now there was a proper trade.)Who'd buy a travel article from me? I kept telling him I had to start somewhere, didn't want a cadetship on a suburban weekly, but I wanted a year off before university. And of course, he couldn't see why I needed to bother with university either. Barry wasn't interested, and it wasn't doing him any harm. He was doing well in the bank.

And that's where Barry still is. A branch manager in a bank in Hertfordshire. And Dad is seven years dead, Mum eight. I don't think either of them ever got used to the prosthesis. And I haven't seen any of them since I farewelled Dad on a railway platform on the way to Gatwick last visit. Wouldn't come to the airport. Too far. Just a stiff wave. Not even a handshake. Guess he thought I'd be back, with my tail between my legs. Mum wouldn't even come out of the house. Although at least she hugged me. Snuffling away the tears, poor thing. I have genuinely missed her the most since.

But never enough to go back. England seems such a miserly place to me now. Wet, miserable people, forever trying to get in out of the rain. Petrified of the snow, even though it comes every year. Hesitant of the sun, although they have no idea what real sun is. Always worried about the trains, or the buses, or the roads. But I am wrong to align my Dad with Barry. Dad was not small-minded. He was a big-picture person. Could see truths and pronounce insight the breadth of which I have never been capable. I guess I miss that. My own shortcoming. I want to keep something positive alive in my memory of him, even if it is to my detriment.

But I don't think I am gay. I keep thinking about it, and the "What if I am" just seems so irrelevant to me. I still want to have sex with Robert again, but I don't actually think of him as attractive. I don't want to have a photograph of him so that I can admire his fabulous aquiline nose or his luscious silver-blond hair or his water-blue eyes. I'm not looking at other men now as 'attractive'. Whereas I still lust after women's bodies endlessly. The older I get, the less discriminate I am. Every breast or rump or set of hips is worthy of attention. Every face I can afford to spend time on without attracting attention. And I still love Mei-ling. That remains a truth for me.

Anyway, after seven years of cat-and-mouse wrangling with the only surviving member of my immediate family, all I have of my father's house is a photocopy of a will that remained resolutely woman-identified in the face of the facts. I have love, and I have a fulfilling future. I want to move on.

*

Table

I almost called Cunningham today. Was on the verge so many times. Kept walking to the phone, picking it up, dialling – even let it ring a couple of times once. But couldn't risk the pick-up. Mei-ling has been ambushed by her Commission. Called to an unscheduled meeting at the offices of the Chair and grilled about her meeting with Lillith Plant before Christmas, and Kendall Chamberlain's jeremiad to the Minister at the opening of *Dream*. Derek Barrimore and Harold Winterbourne were there, obviously embarrassed. And Daphne Barnsworth openly advocating her friend Plant's interests.

What is disturbing is that as members of a governance body they take these 'events' seriously. It is not really their role to hear 'complaints' from disgruntled 'suppliers' – for that's what these contractors are. Their role is to contribute to, understand and advocate the strategy, then support the CEO in delivering it. Mei-ling has been clear with them all along of her vision for the company, and the way in which she intends to achieve it. But these three bail Mei-ling up on the Chair's turf, no secretary, no formal agenda, no minutes taken. Just a concerted grilling from Barnsworth and Winterbourne about allegations made by Plant and Chamberlain concerning Mei-ling's professional conduct and fitness for the job, with Barrimore playing 'honest broker'.

In retrospect, I think Mei-ling should have asked them to place their questions on notice and allow her time to address them in an appropriate manner. She should have then left the meeting and taken the questions to the next Commission meeting, so that it could be minuted. But you don't think of these astute and prudent actions at the time, do you? I know that if it had happened to me, I would have been both so angry and so frightened that I probably would have buckled under and compliantly asked if they wanted my resignation.

Luckily, Mei-ling is not me. She is an amazingly strong and clear-thinking woman. And she took their questions head on. Pointed out to them that she did not need to know anything about design: that was what she employed Chamberlain to do. And she had begun working on the design for *Dream* a full eight months in advance of the production, partly because that was her preferred approach but also because Chamberlain himself had complained to her early on about always being brought in at the last minute, and never being involved as an integral part of the production team. So Mei-ling had involved him in all of the creative meetings with lighting designer and production manager.

It was Chamberlain himself who dithered over a firm design, failed to present a model to the production team at the outset of production prep, and was still asking for changes in the production week. It was this that might explain why he had problems in production week, not his relationship with Mei-ling. And she further pointed out that Kendal Chamberlain was already contracted to work with her on *South Pacific*, and she felt confident he was professional enough to raise any concerns he had with her personally if they were of any real merit.

As for Plant, Mei-ling told them what she had told Plant: that she had been offered a creative slot with the company last year for the first time producing her own promotion, funded to attend the National Tourism Workshop on the company's behalf, and been offered creative roles in two other major King's Company campaigns. She had barely been out of contract with the company the entire year, even though she had her own chain of travel agencies to run.

While she had not been offered a creative director role in the current program of promotional activity, she had been offered other roles and Mei-ling would be sure to place her well amongst the list of contractors she put to the other creative directors in this year's promotional program. Mei-ling met with her before Christmas solely to ask her to either sign a contract for a range of roles in the coming year or not. And she had signed.

As Chair, Barrimore himself had one final card to play. He revealed that Robert was in Singapore, and had learnt that Mei-ling's departure from BHT was not on the crest of the wave she had led them to believe. This, of course, is difficult for Mei-ling to refute outright because it is both true and untrue.

It is true that, in the end, Mei-ling's long-standing strategy of empowering the company to run itself, under the direction of a local appointee, was successful. For the last 6 months, there were concerted approaches by staff and, in the end, a united approach by a strong faction within the organisation to the BHT Board seeking Mei-ling's replacement by a local. They clearly wanted control of the enterprise. I remember how ironic we found it that, for four years, we were treated as cultural tourists by Mei-ling's own profession in Singapore – that was their way of accepting us as 'experts' at the same time as objectifying us as 'foreigners', by continually acting as cultural hosts for us - but in the end we were reduced to cultural imperialists (not that they used that language, of course).

The BHT Board's response was, appropriately, to give face to the 'insurrectionists' by listening to their concerns appropriately and then giving them no further quarter. Management was Mei-ling's domain. And, as Mei-ling pointed out to Barrimore, she gave him her BHT Chair as primary referee, so Barrimore presumably spoke with him as part of Mei-ling's selection process. Mei-ling did not conceal the nature of her departure from BHT. In her interview, however, she naturally focussed on the strengths and successes of her performance. What else would they expect her to do and, really, what business was it of theirs anyway? Nevertheless, it is easy to hear a very real construction of being 'found out' here – Mei-ling is not imagining it. This whole meeting was totally inappropriate.

Despite her evident competence in the event, I think Mei-ling was deeply shocked by the in-grouping, partisan approach taken, and the cloak-and-dagger manner in which the meeting was set up. She was very angry when she came home. I advised her to phone Phillipa to find out if she had any idea what was behind it. It was only then that Mei-ling actually started to cry, as she was explaining to Phillipa over the phone the questions the Commission had asked.

Even more worrying was Phillipa's response. Seemingly supportive at first, and ignorant of the meeting. But then measured in her advice, and not at all warm. Her exact words were, according to Mei-ling: You have to consider carefully how far you want to go with this. It was Mei-ling who had to say: As you can hear, Phillipa, I am very disturbed by this event. But Phillipa seemed unmoved.

That frightens me. While Mei-ling was in Melbourne she ended up in tears one night because Tynan McAvaddy (after firstly trying to con her off) engaged her in a conversation about how she was going to manage at King's Company. She'd been out of the country for a while, he said, and people had moved on or moved around, so who did she know anymore?

He was clearly moving himself into a position to be her contact-broker, because he was trying to interest her in a designer for *South Pacific* he knew from Adelaide. But, after she had evaded his ardours by wishing him goodnight in the hotel lobby, she went out again into the streets of Melbourne, and found herself sobbing in despair. For a moment, she says, she was overwhelmed with the magnitude of her task: who **did** she know?

And yet, I reminded her, she knew so many. Had already been in contact with so many. They were just not the creative talent or agency managers the other state heads knew. Not members of the in-group. Not cultural currency. But, of course, far more 'cultural' in currency. That was Mei-ling's strength. Cultural tourism was where she led, and that was why she was in the position she was. She was a pioneer. The others were part of an old guard.

But it worried me that a man who has himself only just joined the company, and as a production manager rather than part of the creative team, should make so confronting and bold a proposition. How is it his business? And then this destabilising behaviour from her Commission and, I hate to say it, Phillipa herself. There must be another agenda. I can't help looking at the "Tourrorist Invasion" headlines we're getting almost every second week now in the press and wondering whether the Cooksland State Government are getting cold feet. But then, how would a newcomer like McAvaddy know about that?

Anyway, it's nice that she can still find such joy in time with Rose, who took her up the back garden in the dusk to show her the magic mushroom. The 'dominant member of the pack' has just literally 'mushroomed' out of sight. I've never seen anything like it. Rose can almost sit under its 'helmet'. Mei-ling says we should get someone in to assess it. Might have chanced upon a rare species. But that was later. With Rose, she just sat there in the dusk, exchanging stories about the fairies that must live around so magic a mushroom.

She's gone off to work today in a putting-it-behind-me frame of mind. But I haven't slept. I feel so betrayed by Robert. He didn't mention he was going to Singapore when we last 'met'. Yet he seems happy to dump on Mei-ling and, by default, me, behind our backs. Perhaps he's miffed that I haven't contacted him since our last 'meeting'. But then, he hasn't rung me either. Perhaps it was just a one off for him after all. Perhaps he really does do that sort of thing all the time, and I am alone with this. But if he's put one 'trump card' on the table, presumably to further his own ends, what's to stop him playing another? Makes me feel sick to the heart to even think of it.

*

I hope this is an act of fateful retribution, but the police have raided various premises occupied by Nimrod Hannah and Kendell Chamberlain, impounded computers and 'detained' the pair to 'assist police with their inquiries' after 'reliable intelligence' of a plot to bring terrorists and refugees into Australia virtually using alternative cultural tourism ventures. A creepy development of the 'tour-r-r-rism' thing – which I had thought politicians might allow to die a thankful death – but I'm glad Hannah in particular got what he had coming. Dashedly patriarchal, what.

*

Curtains

In the theatre, they talk about 'curtain up' and 'curtain down' as a kind-of code for the beginning and end of 'the performance'. When you think about it, that's how we use curtains in our lives: closing them marks the end of 'the day', opening them marks the beginning of 'the next day' or 'the new day'. So is it coincidence that Mei-ling thought it an appropriate time, after dropping Rose off at her new kindy, to buy her some new curtains; to mark not only the beginning of a new phase in Rose's life, but also a new phase in ours? For we now pass beyond that period in which we are the sole and primary 'significant adults' in Rose's life. Now she comes under the influence of others, and will enter into relationships with peers of whom we have no knowledge.

We were going to have a coffee on the way, because we were feeling a little fragile about all of this – and, of course, it was a rare opportunity for Mei-ling and I to have time together in a way we used to before Rose was born. But as we were approaching the café I had in mind, I lent forward to see if there were any tables, and who should be at the table closest to the kerbside but Phillipa Hay deep in conversation with Harold Winterbourne. Less than a week after her conversation with Mei-ling about the Commission's ambush, there was Phillipa with one of the main antagonists.

Even in the moment I reasoned: perhaps she is adopting her usual approach of building bridges through personal contact and conversation. Phillipa can be a good bridge-builder and networker. But then, why hasn't she told Mei-ling she intends to do this? Why didn't she say in a conversation with Mei-ling during the intervening period that she would talk to Harold Winterbourne to find out what was going on? Or that she was having breakfast with him tomorrow and would raise the matter with him? Or perhaps it was just a chance invitation or meeting that occurred that morning.

This reasoning happened in microseconds, as the car approached and I identified them. And even as I was rationalising, another part of me wanted to make our presence known. As if a part of my mind I don't know very well, but which is closer to my bodily intelligence (if there is such a thing), had already seen a way of testing the various hypotheses my rational consciousness was sorting through. If we were seen, Phillipa would have to raise it with Mei-ling. Or not, as the case may be. Depending on her allegiances. She would feel forced to declare her hand. Or not.

And so, even as I we were passing, and I was saying to Mei-ling "It's Phillipa, with Winterbourne! It is! Look!" Mei-ling tried not to look. But I was leaning forward over the wheel and gesturing with exaggeration, pointing across the wheel. As Mei-ling was trying to maintain her face and anonymity, I was the monkey clambering around the car's interior aping "Look at me! Look at me!"

It was such a bizarre contradiction, the interior of our car at that moment. Mei-ling manifesting a most uncharacteristic yet obviously atavistic Chineseness, and me regressing into an almost obscenely infantile masculinity. And so we were, in that second as our vehicle sailed passed Harold Winterbourne and Phillipa Hay seated at a table of an al fresco café in Westside, and Phillipa's eyes glanced in my direction, returned to Winterbourne in slow motion, and Winterbourne's eyes followed hers in our direction as I yanked my head around to watch, still acclaiming their presence loudly to Mei-ling. But he did not want to be seen seeing us. Nor did Phillipa. No bright and cheery wave we would have received this time 12 months ago.

I could have been wrong, of course. I could still be wrong. But I will be interested to learn tonight whether or not Phillipa raises the sighting, or her meeting with Winterbourne, during the day. I almost wonder if I should talk to Phillipa myself. Mei-ling asked, after we had passed, did they see us? I lied, and said I wasn't sure. And she asked me why I had pointed. And I avoided answering. I avoided saying: because I wanted them to know we had seen them. Because I know that I have intervened, even if only in a minor way, in an event which is not mine to interfere with. This is Mei-ling's business.

But I know Phillipa. I have known her for longer than I have known Mei-ling. The unappealing immanence of betrayal that bolted from within me in the car, in that moment, was unavoidable. I acted. And I fear so much the potential of that intervention. And I can't extricate it from an association with my sense that I have already betrayed Mei-ling, with Robert Cunningham. That there is something self-destructive in me that I don't properly understand. And a fear that this might get out of control.

But this instance, I reason, *is* different from Cunningham. Traditionally I have invested my energies solely in supporting Mei-ling. Now I have pushed myself in there. If relations between Mei-ling and her Commission deteriorate further, it may be my fault. And I am already concealing my role from Mei-ling, even though I don't even know that it *is* a role: that I have actually been seen by Phillipa and Winterbourne making my point. I may, after all, still remain just the faithful adviser on the edge of somebody else's story. But still there is that uncomfortable self-doubt.

Either way, our subsequent coffee conversation became about what might be going on politically between Cooksland Arts and the King's Company Commission, and what Phillipa's role in it might be, as opposed to a debrief on what had been a rather beautiful moment barely minutes earlier, when we had slipped away from our daughter, having placed her for the first time in the caring hands of an institutional program of education that will fashion her life for the next ten to fifteen years or more. Crossing that threshold into the next room and releasing her at the same time, letting her go on a journey of individuation we can no longer protect her from, and she going so willingly. Moving around the kindergarten from box to box, play area to play area, so much more to look at and do than in our small house, and people her size and age to do it with.

And we stay for a while, feeling redundant already. And when we stoop to say goodbye, she is pulling aside the curtain to one of the low shelving areas, ready to pull out whatever lies beyond. She looks up at us, her mind already engaged in the next act, and is perfectly happy that we are leaving. Confident we will return.

I couldn't help thinking of that first time Mei-ling and I brought her home from the hospital as a newborn. We placed her into her bassinette in the room we (mostly Mei-ling) had so lovingly prepared for her, and sat on the bed she would one day sleep in, listened to the traffic of a hot and humid Singapore passing through the streets below our apartment, held hands and wept. We didn't know what to do next. So it was when we sat in the car this morning, looking back across at the kindergarten, holding hands and crying.

*

Stumps

Robert was bold enough to show his face today. I was underneath the house, hanging out washing between the stumps and pushing Rose on the swing. I felt my heart race when I saw him moving from the front steps around the side of the house. I knew it was him, but couldn't bring myself to look. On one hand the emotions released when we had sex were rushing up to claim my head once more, and on the other was my anger at him for going behind Mei-ling's back to BHT in Singapore. It was Rose who greeted him as he appeared in the driveaway. And he who greeted her back with the usual enthusiasm he reserved for her.

"How's the mushroom?" he asked her cheerfully.

"Bigger," Rose replied with pride.

I expected him to be brazen, that same boyish grin and hail-fellow-well-met "Hi!" of his, as if nothing was wrong. But instead his greeting to me, as he looked up from Rose, was softer; almost apologetic, seeking forgiveness. A disposition that enabled me to straightaway take the upper hand. "You've got a nerve, coming round here."

"It wasn't my fault," he said, rising and coming closer to me, anxious for Rose. "They asked me to go. Bumiputra Huayu Tamil. Wanted to go where Mei-ling was taking King's Company. Thought it was a great strategy but wanted to understand it better. Didn't want to see ignorant to Mei-Ling's face.

"I didn't understand why they approached me. I knew it felt odd. But I was pissed off with Dale, and thought: goody! A free trip to Singapore! I knew I hadn't even undertaken the business development consultancy for Mei-ling that they had been told I had. I mean, the work I did with her was didn't even result in a formal report. But I took up the offer anyway.

"Found out the rest when I got there. It wasn't until I came back, and Winterbourne and Barrimore invited me to lunch, ostensibly for a debrief to learn what I had discovered on my trip, that I in turn leant who it was that had recommended me for the job in the first place. And frankly, if Mei-ling's days are numbered, well I wouldn't mind being on the right side. Sorry."

"So who was it? Recommended you."

"And for Singapore. Who do you think? Hay of course."

I was quite disarmed. Still angry, but he had declared his hand so evenly. I couldn't reproach him. I told him I wasn't aware Mei-ling's days were quite so well numbered. Suggested he talk to her, as she was the one who needed to know. He said he wasn't sure he could. But he wanted to square it with me, because, well just because.

He did not stay much beyond that. Asked me whether I was OK. I told him I wasn't sure what that meant. He turned to go, and then turned back again. Look, he said, it wasn't ... And I could see tears starting to well up in his eyes. I didn't ... he tried again. But couldn't finish his sentence. And I had no desire to help him. "You're not easy, David," he said finally, and the tears dropped from his eyes. "Has that occurred to you? I didn't know whether to ring you or call round or ... I just didn't know."

He looked at me a moment longer, but I didn't know what to say in reply. So he turned to Rose and gave her a little cute half-scratching-the-air sort of wave adults give to babies. "Bye cutey," he said with a forced smile, and left.

It was Rose who named it. "Robert's crying," she said. And I was confused again. It was easier when I could simply distrust him, stereotype him as the betrayer. Now everything is simply complex again. God knows what I'll do if Rose mentions it to Mei-ling.

*

Rose did tell Mei-ling. In her inimitably unguarded way. As Mei-ling was putting her to bed. Robert was here today, she told her mum; he was crying.

And of course I had not mentioned Robert's visit to Mei-ling. Oh yes, I responded dismissively, as if I'd forgotten. He didn't stay

159

long. We were hanging out the washing. He was upset. Kept saying he just wanted to check we were okay, but wouldn't go on. And I couldn't face him, frankly. Guilty about dobbing you in to the King's Company Commission, I imagine.. Or because he fancies you, Mei-ling countered, but coyly. "I doubt that," I said, half laughing, hoping she wouldn't see my unsureness of footing. Oh I don't know, she said, her head cocked on one side with that quizzical, mocking look her Asian eyelids don't quite allow her to pull off; I think I'd still fancy you if I were gay.

And we laughed, and had a cuddle and a kiss. But we didn't make love. And of course I still don't know whether she knows, or how she knows if she does. My brief peccadillo with Robert Cunningham has placed an internal injunction between myself and my partner. How do I tell her what I know about Phillipa Hay? I am, as they say in cricket, stumped.

*

Plates

I may owe Phillipa an apology. She has delivered on a long-standing promise to introduce us to the new federal Republican candidate for King, Bevan Steele. Bevan used to be a diplomat in Kuala Lumpur, and has a daughter Rose's age, and Phillipa has been saying for ages we would have something in common. So it looks like she might be genuinely trying to build political bridges for Mei-ling after all. During the course of the evening, for instance, she opened up a discussion about Max Kingsbury and Doug Dingwall and the impasses over the Next Stage. Bevan smiled with one of those "Ah, so that's what this is about" nods, but very open to the discussion. Everything, it seems, is to be expected in politics.

He meted out a briefing to us as if he were distributing plates at the dining table. Each one with a different course of the meal on it. Dingwall, he said, is politically very astute, but intellectually not particularly committed to much – which I took to be a polite way of saying he was short of a few. It was well known, however, that the Tourism and Arts Minister saw himself as Deputy Premier material and was interested in neither Tourism nor the Arts. But he had got himself into a bind over the Performance Centre because he had promised cabinet it would pay for itself within three years, and it was not going to even come close. Hence his initial enthusiasm for the tourism-subsidises-arts thrust of Mei-ling's application to King's Company. Kingsbury was still playing the commercial potential of the centre for all it was worth in order to strengthen his position. Kingsbury also had the ear of the Premier.

The King's Company was, by comparison, small fry, and a drain on government because of its seeming dependence on subsidy, even if only in this 'start-up' phase. If Mei-ling could remind Dingwall that the commercial solution to the Next Stage lay with Kings Company, and a tourism–led business model, not with Kingsbury and his performing arts-led model, she might give him something to take back to cabinet. Bevan also suggested Dingwall had a healthy ego, which could sustain a great deal of stroking without blenching.

I asked him whether the federal government's 'terrorism' backlash against tourism was a factor here: whether the state government was considering revising its commitment to the King's Company strategy, even though cultural rather than mainstream tourism was its platform. Steele acknowledged there was a potential impact. International visitor days for the coming year were already suffering. And the spread of police action linking terrorism to tourism was disturbing. But he knew the

Premier personally and a policy change was not on his radar at the moment.

It was a convivial evening. Rose and the Steeles daughter played happily until they grew sleepy. Bevan and Mei-ling were able to share anecdotes and views about the stresses and pitfalls of working cross-culturally with both the Malays and the Chinese Malays. As a diplomat, Bevan proved less tolerant of face than Mei-ling. In the end, he said, you called their bluff, stared them down. Whereas Mei-ling went the face route to the bitter end (literally, in the case of BHT).

Phillipa brought Tynan McAvaddy as her partner for the night (his family are still in Adelaide), which provided Mei-ling with a further social opportunity to get to know him better. But seeing Phillipa with Winterbourne still flips across my mind's eye from time to time. She has never mentioned it to Mei-ling. Maybe I should ask her myself; although it's probably a bit late now. And anyway, they might not have seen us at all.

I think back over an evening like this, and try to place Robert Cunningham in it. He could be a gossip, or a commentator on it for another group – his own sub-culture, perhaps – but he doesn't have a place in his own right. Which means he doesn't have a place in the political world inhabited by Bevan Steele and, by association, Phillipa. For some reason I draw comfort from that. Feel less exposed.

*

Kitchen

I've worked out who Phillipa was talking about that evening on our front veranda. She is having an affair with Tynan McAvaddy! Miriam Oakwood, Mei-ling's new resident designer from Melbourne (another step towards a functioning staff complement), was getting a lift back to her hotel with Phillipa last night – she's doing costumes and graphic design for Kendall Chamberlain on *South Pacific* – and Phillipa, without explanation, just had to go 'via home' for some reason. Well, who should be waiting outside when she 'popped in' but McAvaddy with – wait for it - some *fish*. He'd been out fishing and so had brought Phillipa some round. Lucky she had stopped by!

She let him in to leave them on the kitchen table, and then proceeded on with Miriam. This is like eleven o'clock at night. McAvaddy's family have only been here a fortnight! I can't imagine how he explains this to his wife. Oh dear, she's just been *so* supportive during this first couple of months! I just *had* to share some of the flathead with her. Mei-ling had Miriam around for tea tonight. They were pissing themselves about it. Now I understand why Phillipa's Sunday morning outings with Rose have ceased!

*

Bed

I can't escape an image in my mind of Mei-ling sitting up in bed this morning. She was surrounded with texts, floor plan and designs for *South Pacific*, for which she is in the middle of production. In her mind, she is pulling it all together for the final run up to the show. And Phillipa is on the phone, because

Chamberlain and Hannah are unhappy with the contract arrangements for their September promotion. In her mind, Mei-ling has told Phillipa to arrange these months ago. She has actually spoken to their new shared PA, Kerry Charnell about them. But Charnell has not issued the contracts because, she says, Phillipa was uncertain they were proceeding with them.

Chamberlain and Hannah have their own company, the administrator of which has phoned Mei-ling at home direct because Charnell gave him her home number. So Me-ling phones Phillipa, but gets Charnell because Phillipa is unavailable. Finally Phillipa phones back; she was over at the Department in a meeting. What about? Oh, just something, what's the problem? Mei-ling explains. Phillipa had not thought they were contracting them. Didn't Mei-ling remember? Under the new IR laws, employers only need a verbal contract. They discussed this.

Yes, but Mei-ling remembers saying that they had their own company, and to go with what they wanted. Now their administrator says Hannah and Chamberlain are threatening to pull out.

Well what can she do about that, says Phillipa? It's just as likely to be because of their entanglement with the police, which remains unresolved. They have equipment still impounded. Maybe they simply can't complete the job. And around it goes.

It is actually Mei-ling who herself rings Hannah and Chamberlain individually to discuss their concerns with them. They want contracts, of course they do, why wouldn't they? She will see to it. It is harder with Chamberlain because he is also objecting to Miriam's involvement in *South Pacific* – never saw the reason for her in the first place.

I can't believe this guy has no sense of shame. As if all that is happening to him politic-legally just isn't a factor; he just wants what he wants. Admittedly for a pair that have made such an art of disdaining the 'conventional' tourism industry, they have received an overwhelming show of professional outrage at their 'persecution' from the profession. But it just seems to have buoyed their aesthetic egotism and sense of superiority. Anyway, Mei-ling rings their administrator, tells him it will happen. Rings Phillipa, instructs her to proceed with the contracts.

Phillipa's news then is that neither Sydney nor Melbourne has taken up their offer of *South Pacific*. Apparently Mei-ling left the running on this too late; even though she has had the promotion on the table of the state creative directors' forum since she announced her season last October, and discussed it with the CD's of both state commissions in Melbourne in January. Mei-ling had expected Phillipa to follow up, again to firm up contracts but, says Phillipa, she hadn't understood this. I know Mei-ling sits down with Phillipa and talks these plans through in detail. I have seen them doing it when Rose and I arrive during the course of the day, or to pick Mei-ling up of an evening.

At the same time Alicia Driffield is on the phone. Does Mei-ling remember she has a sponsorship deal with Southgate Energy, who want to sponsor a schools touring version of *South Pacific*? This is low on Mei-ling's horizon, because again she has asked Phillipa to pull it together. Phillipa should remember how to do this. That was what she was doing when she and Mei-ling first met: extracting school touring versions of interactive cultural tourism promotions for Surrey Street. It's not hard to do, and is the sort of thing that can be undertaken once *South Pacific* is in performance. But Phillipa has done nothing, and clearly given Alicia the impression it is Mei-ling's responsibility.

Mei-ling knows who she will approach amongst the talent, but Alicia is talking about withdrawing the sponsorship deal now because she will have nobody to introduce the Southgate delegation to on opening night. She says Southgate are already nervous because of the terrorism~tourism backlash, particularly in rural. Well, the Chair of Kings Company would be a good start, Mei-ling suggests; and perhaps the Minister. But they want to meet the talent, says Alicia. And so they will, says Mei-ling, there will be an extravaganza full of them, all looking forward to the drinks afterwards. Surely Alicia could introduce the Southgate execs to a selection? Mei-ling doesn't sound arch, ever 'faceful', but her irritation is embedded in the question.

And there I am, playing with Rose in the lounge, 'talking' her glove puppets. While this bizarre world of neo-crisis wheels around Mei-ling's head conjured up by King's telephone towers, and the firmer foundations of text lay about her on the counterpane awaiting final assembly. Talk about holding the universe together.

*

Title Deeds

Connell argues that practice is an underrated feature of social action that has more of an explanatory role in the workings of power than many of the structural and functional characteristics normally valued by social analysts. And I look at the increasing number of smokers gathering around the downpipes exterior to the buildings in which they work and think: so how long is it before they become a proletariat? It's not a very serious thought, of course. But it certainly is a dividing feature of the Kings Company office culture. Whenever Rose and I arrive early enough to find the majority of the staff still there, it is easy to spot group who gather on the veranda overlooking the King River for their lung-filling fix of tobacco and oral stimulation.

166

Phillipa is the main protagonist. Invariably joined by Alicia and, more recently, Tynan and Kerry Charnell. It's not a conspiracy. But the practice that brings them together also separates them from the rest of the staff, and includes conversation that the rest are not party to but, rather, observe through the floor-to-ceiling glass between them. They become a distinct in-group, where no other exists. Even the executive team do not function as an in-group by virtue of any one shared practice or physical site for it.

Certainly that was where Harold Winterbourne found Phillipa yesterday afternoon, when he and Derek Barrimore returned with Mei-ling all-of-a-lather after a meeting with Max Kingsbury. Kingsbury had brought together all of the other local users of the Next Stage he could imagine for a 'stakeholders discussion on' potential hiring demand. Of course the tactic pushed Kings Company back into the 'preferred hirer' category, just one amongst many, and Kingsbury was able to manufacture a potential demand that fenced Kings Company into a smaller and smaller band of occupancy.

Winterbourne was particularly flustered by this tactic because the Department had no forewarning of it, and if Kingsbury reported the outcome direct to the Minister he, as the bureaucrat responsible for the Tourism~Arts strategy, would have to manage it. So according to Mei-ling, he was all "Well that was a disaster" and "What are we going to do now?", and because Barrimore did not understand government bureaucracy or performing arts politics, he bought into the impression they were 'in a fix'.

Mei-ling of course was neither angered nor flustered. She was used to Kingsbury by now: it was clearly a tactic, and they had to come up with a way around him. She had spent the meeting redefining appropriative line from Kingsbury into one of her own, as in, to the client rather than Kingsbury: "Well of course King's Company will wish to accommodate your needs. Collaboration is what this strategy is about." And "This is new, it is risky, but not to you. To your company it brings stability." She sat down with Barrimore to talk through tactical and, if necessary, strategic options. When Winterbourne returned, much calmer, he had found Phillipa on the veranda, smoking a cigarette, as calm as the day, he said, a 'wise buddha'. She had the solution. Talk to the Minister.

This was what actually infuriated Mei-ling, because it was one of the options she was about to propose to her Chair, based on Bevan Steele's advice, and now here it was presented by another Commission member as if it was the only solution, and one presented by another member of the management team than its CEO. Again, an example of a Commission member unable to separate out their governance role from their social and other professional relationships. He still thinks of Phillipa as the able deputy director that used to work for him in Tourism and the Arts. And now a supposedly trusted senior manager with King's Company, acting outside the executive, exploiting a direct route to governance, rather than pursuing it through the CEO as is appropriate.

I'm still thinking I should talk to Phillipa. It was on my recommendation, I feel, that Mei-ling took her on. It was I who took their relationship beyond the workplace at Surrey Street, because I knew Phillipa from university. But it's becoming hard to know where to start. So much of the conversation now would begin from a position of suspicion: why did you do this, what were you talking about with so-and-so, are you aware this is how this set of actions is being perceived, did you really not understand such-and-such? It may be that Phillipa is simply incompetent, in which case I would not want to offend her. But, as Cunningham had intimated, she may also be working against Mei-ling; in which case, she is doing so fairly incisively, and I'm not sure I could trust her enough to discuss anything with her really.

And then of course there is the possibility that she has talked with Cunningham and knows of my indiscretion. She could be just waiting for me to open up a conversation with her 'outside the ring', so that she can insert that particular knife to immobilise me. I wouldn't be able to talk to Mei-ling about anything I learned from Phillipa, because Phillipa would 'blow my cover' re-Robert.

And then there is still Robert himself. It would be so easy for him to reveal our 'encounter'. No skin off his nose – although he still appears to be with Dale, so may not want to compromise himself either.

This is conjecture, all of it. But I feel paralysed into inertia. Keep trying to focus on my primary role, which is to support Mei-ling. I am starting to become genuinely worried about her situation. There are so many external demands, without the internal stressors becoming unmanageable also.

Phillipa is in sufficient a position of trust to be able to undermine just about anything Mei-ling might wish to succeed, if she so desires. But there is nothing I can do beyond the house, as it were, to influence her situation that might not also add to Mei-ling's burdens. The best I can do is remain on the inside of our 'home', and support my love from there. Hold the house together, as it were. As best I can.

*

Dining Room

It's funny, when Bevan Steele advised Mei-ling to stroke Doug Dingwall's ego, it was inoffensive and vaguely amusing. But when Doug Dingwall advises Mei-ling to do the same to Max Kingsbury, it is outrageous.

Both conversations took place in private. But Steele was objectifying Dingwall as someone with an ego capable of sustaining considerable attention, sharing the fact sardonically with Mei-ling as an equal. Whereas Dingwall was objectifying Kingsbury as a powerful object whose power needs to be undermined by feminine artfulness. In so-doing, he was also objectifying Mei-ling as less powerful because she is a woman, with but a 'woman's power' to use, her 'charms'.

It is unbelievable that a man in this day and age thinks he can get away with such flagrant sexism. This is a man in a position of considerable power and authority. And he made the suggestion, according to Mei-ling, with a sort of smirking self-effacement that attempted to make it clear that he knew he was being sexist, but that it was a 'tactic' Mei-ling should consider anyway. She looked at Barrimore. She looked at Winterbourne. Winterbourne sniggered with the Minister. Barrimore was impassive, but there was a glint in his eye for Mei-ling. Three men. One woman.

According to Mei-ling, Dingwall began the meeting atrociously by ostentatiously 'tasting' the stelvin capped (so it couldn't possibly be corked) *Chateau* non-alcoholic wine he had served with their lunch. In a private dining room at Parliament house. So this was Winterbourne's solution, as handed to him by Phillipa Hay.

As it was, Mei-ling almost missed the meeting anyway, because Kerry Charnell had again put the appointment in Mei-ling's diary at the wrong time. This is now a consistent pattern of error. But when Mei-ling complains to Phillipa, Phillipa (who poached Charnell from her old Department in government) says she does not have a problem with her. Round and round. Round and round.

Dingwall also placed the terrorism~cultural tourism threat on the table formally for the first time. But not as something to discuss strategically but, rather, in wistful, musing manner of: well, Mei-ling, you'd better be careful or 'events' may just wrest your 'jewel' from you. Tourism numbers are already down on the coast – as if this has anything to do with cultural tourism and the long-term viability of the King's Company strategy. Just so wet.

*

Fence

Way has interned his first batch of tourists under counter terrorism legislation. The Senate review has barely started. One of Lillith Plant's travel agents has already suggested to Mei-ling that the detention centre (which is out bush somewhere) would make an ideal cultural tourism destination. We can only guess that he is winding Mei-ling up. A detention centre certainly would require some redefinition of the terms 'culture' and 'community' for tourism purposes! But the mere suggestion highlights how dangerous this particular bear in the market place is for Mei-ling.

*

Ceiling

Phillipa has finally revealed her full hand. She has led the executive management team against Mei-ling in a direct approach to the Commission. And, to make matters worse, the Commission actually agreed to meet with them. The Commission had a lawyer present, and the managers (Alicia, Tynan and Phillipa) also had a lawyer present. All unbeknown to Mei-ling.

The meeting took place off-site, in Barrimore's offices. The first Mei-ling knew about it was when Barrimore and Winterbourne walked into her office and informed her that the full Commission wanted to meet with her; at a meeting set down for when? On her birthday, of course. When else? This is at 5pm, just two hours before Mei-ling has to front up for the first night of *South Pacific*. They are lucky to find her there at all – she has been in the theatre all day, still trying to sort out difficulties with Chamberlain's design. She has to go home and get changed. No time even for tea. And no inclination now to eat anything anyway.

There is a raft of 'charges'. Mei-ling's failure to deliver on the Southgate sponsorship. Her mismanagement of the Chamberlain/Hannah contracts. Chamberlain's and Plant's complaints. The disbanding of Bower Bird and subsequent loss of income. Inability to forecast finances because of insecurity over the Next Stage. Cost overrun on the temporary housing of the workshop. Bad press. Mei-ling's personal tardiness – she keeps missing meetings, almost missed one with the Minister. It's such a fit up.

I think Mei-ling's a bit shell shocked. I certainly am. The governance body have no business meeting with staff, let alone hearing complaint from them. In doing so they simply abrogate their right to continue as a Commission with any legitimate governance role. They have 'become' the CEO. It is insane. And of course Mei-ling has explanations for every 'charge', but is now placed in a situation where each explanation is exactly that: it can be nothing other than a defence.

But Mei-ling came home, got dressed, and I stepped out with her in my brogues. Jennifer babysat, and had already heard the news. So much for Commission confidentiality. And Mei-ling hosted the Minister, who continued to smirk, and delivered her speech praising all who merited praising – omitting, for the first time, her executive management team. Maintaining face throughout. Came home, drank a bit. But did not weep. Or rail. There is a core of anger deep at her centre that will not let this go. And yet this morning, she is in bed, playing with Rose, full of love and that seemingly endless capacity to enter into relationship. And later on, once she is dressed, goes out to sit under the giant magic mushroom with her.

What makes it worse for me was that, during the drinks after the show, while Mei-ling was engaged with Southgate and the Minister, Winterbourne sidled up to me and struck up a conversation. On the surface, this is not unusual. Even though he is a Board member, at these functions he is essentially a government bureaucrat, so it is not unexpected for one 'ringsider' to consort with another whilst observing the 'main game'. It was the content of his conversation that I found so disturbing, because it confirmed my fears.

How was I finding parenthood? he wanted to know. I said I was enjoying it, and then he asked whether Mei-ling was finding enough time for Rose? I said she made the most of what time she had but no – and perhaps I was too off-guard here, wanting the conversation to work – I didn't think she felt she had enough time with Rose.

Was she thinking of having a second child? he then asked innocently. I said I thought she was pretty committed to her current contract, and the strategy that formed the basis of it, which she very much wanted to see through to a successful completion. Was I sure it would be successful? Yes of course, why wouldn't it be? Everything was on track in terms of her and King's Company's performance.

So what about me, he asked: did I want another child? And when I hesitated, he feigned a grimace. I'm sorry, he said, I am assuming you are actually Rose's biological father. One should not assume such things these days.

So there was the nub. Exploiting his age difference for a clearly intended insinuation. Why would I be a committed partner to Mei-ling and yet not the father of her child? Glancing back at me sideways, the way Robert Cunningham might. A man who 'knows' something I should be wary of. IS the insinuation that Mei-ling is having an affair? Or, more likely, that he knows something about Cunningham and me? That I could not be Rose's father because I am gay?

I managed to reply calmly, with a wry smile, that the last I knew of it I was. In retrospect I should have gone on to innocently raise the coffee meeting we had observed him having with Phillipa, to observe his reaction. But frankly he was scaring the living daylights out of me.

So this has become officially unbelievable from my perspective. And yet it is real. You read about it happening to others, but cannot imagine what it is like to be inside. Where I once craved the sight of Robert Cunningham striding up the path to our house, now I dread it. Anger on Mei-ling's behalf impels me to defend her in some way, but I am petrified Phillipa and Winterbourne have Cunningham in the wings just waiting for me.

I abhor my implication in the net of deceit and misrepresentation that is closing in around Mei-ling, yet feel powerless to help because of it. All I have is an idea of a house I strive to hold together, for her sake. For Rose's sake. But like (yet unlike) blind Samson between the columns, fearing being found out for all my life, for I will bring it down if I need to. For my family's sake.

I remember just after uni, Phillipa was going out with a mate of mine, Sam. They seemed made for each other, and then she broke it off. The reason Phillipa gave was the way his breath smelt when he woke up in the morning and wanted to make love. She'd lived with him for six months, but had chosen to break up with him rather than tell him. I remember Sam was hurt, but more because he was so completely disempowered. Reduced to bad breath: what could be worse? "I mean, are we adults or what?" he complained to me. It remains, it seems, a good question.

*

Religion

I have always enjoyed listening for the bells on Sunday morning, and playing Church music on the hi-fi. I still find the solipsist in me unable to believe in anything for which there is a rational or empirical explanation. I remain unable to forgive Christianity for its role in condoning and supporting fundamental moral wrongs, such as war and usury. But a church for me remains a place of great peace and meditation, particularly when it is empty. It represents the commitment of people to their sense of community, to what they can accomplish together. I continue fundamentally to believe in community, and the strength of consensus and joint action. Even at a time like this. Perhaps even more so at a time like this.

I had not realised I was looking for a church until I spotted one, yesterday morning, near our favourite playground and 'green bit'. It is a small white weatherboard affair, simple inside, all of that lovely wood latticework and pews. I went there this morning, after dropping Rose off at kindy. I wanted to ask for help for Mei-ling, just as I had once wanted to thank somebody or something on the day after Rose's birth in Singapore.

Mei-ling has contracted a lawyer, on Jane Barrimore's advice. Subscriptions for her second year's program of promotional events are the highest ever for King's Company. *South Pacific* was a sell-out. As with *Dream*, the whole concept of adapting an existing performing arts 'work' to carry a cultural tourism message found massive popular acceptance. Mei-ling now has a small ensemble of talent working pretty much permanently with the company, mostly made up of new graduates but with a few of King's industry diehards who are prepared to embrace something new and exciting, run the gauntlet of the old guard opinion leaders. Even a few of the performing arts talent are becoming interested.

The company continues to receive good press, with the sole exception of Mei-ling's work – which we know from box office is in fact fine. The reviews of *South Pacific* are bordering on positive. Even Charlotte Chambers is finding it difficult to find fault. Eventually, the locally spurned antagonists will settle down, and Mei-ling's direction and strategy will prevail. The company is well placed to move into its own home, if the politics can be sorted. Mei-ling is not committed to the rural objectives in her strategy until year three, by which time the Way *Tour-r-rism* 'waves' will have washed away. She is essentially doing well.

And yet in yesterday's paper Ranald Whippet, in town with a National Tourism Commission promotion he had wanted to on-sell to Mei-ling, presented now instead by Kingsbury (so he's buying into the tourism-led arts agenda anyway), openly commented on Mei-ling, saying that, well, she's been 'out of the culture for five years', she 'can't be expected to pick up the threads again instantly', and that 'relationships are important'.

And of course I remember where I have heard that before. Whilst hanging paintings in our lounge room with Robert Cunningham, back in the days when I was glad to meet a man I could talk to. And of course Whippet is gay. So Robert too finally reveals his agenda. I don't know how to protect Mei-ling any more. My guilt is something that just continues to rise within me, like vomit that won't actually commit itself to the emetic, but keeps creeping up and thickening in my throat.

My only redemption lies in hearing that Whippet has been called to front the Senate Tribunal on the Terrorist Impact of Tourism in Australia, to defend the National Tourism Commission from the accusation of pro-terrorist activity. But even that has a sour taste to it: a hope that Mei-ling and authentic cultural tourism will win out because the fabricators lose, rather than on her own merits. And he'll just bullshit his way through it anyway.

How can it come to this? There must be a central action of fairness somewhere in this that will hold out. Surely evidence and rationality carry some currency in a reasonable society that is not directly under an evident threat. Or even an invisible one, such as the elusive and as yet totally non-evident terrorist tourists. Illegal immigrants yes – far more common than even the so-called 'boat people'. But terrorism?

*

Health

I thought I was terrified of Robert Cunningham, but that pales in comparison to the last 24 hours. The way danger can grow so imperceptibly that its immanence is not apparent until it precipitates as crisis.

We've had Rose to the doctor a couple of times in the past few months with her breathing, but it's never been anything radical. Just a tightness in the upper chest that you can hear. I'm terrified of pneumonia, of course, along with meningitis and – well, she's a bit old for SIDS now.

On Tuesday it was the same diagnosis. A mild asthma. Nothing to worry about. No infection. Then yesterday morning she really seemed to be having difficulty with her breathing. I could hear it in the chest and throat. I found her out under the giant mushroom, sitting against the – well, trunk it seems now. (Still soft and fungussy, but trunk in thickness.) I encouraged her to come in to wish mummy happy birthday. Kept asking her: are you okay? She kept nodding. But how would Rose know if her life was in danger? At what temperature does the frog jump out of the boiling water?

It still seemed alright at that stage. Mei-ling opens her presents and Rose understands well now that it is Mummy's birthday, even that she and I are giving Mummy a special present from us both. And Mei-ling enjoys the time in bed with Rose, playing with the wrapping paper and the presents she has received. Then Rose and I set about the morning, while Mei-ling looks through her notes for a few minutes in preparation for her Commission meeting that night.

But when I next look at Rose I think: she's grey. I ask her again, is she okay? She is listless, sitting down and leaning back against a wall. Her breathing seems very constrained. I bring Mei-ling to her. Mei-ling is worried too. We ring the doctor, who asks us to describe her symptoms. He remembers her from the day before. Bring her straight round, he says, he will meet us out the front. This sounds serious. Luckily, he is just around the corner.

By now we are carrying Rose. The doctor doesn't even get her out of the car. Examines her there and says, almost immediately, take her straight to the Women's and Children's. He will ring ahead. The practice nurse comes with us in the car. I can't believe this is happening. Rose is actually starting to turn blue. It is an acute asthma attack, he says. Suddenly, I am just so frightened. I don't drive like a maniac, but I drive steadily and insistently. I have my headlights and my hazards on and drive (slowly) through red lights, sounding my horn. Right down the main street from East King towards the hospital.

I forget Cunningham. I forget Hay. I forget the entire Commission of the King's Company and their folly, Plant, De Leon and the doyens of Cooksland tourism, the skulduggery of Tynan McAvaddy, Max Kingsbury and the performing arts lobby, Doug Dingwall – the entire petty-political morass just falls away from my mind as the car moves forward. Terrorist tourism isn't even at the edge of a synapse. All I can think of is the road in front of me, the cars and pedestrians on it, and how I can get through them before Rose dies. Miraculously other drivers seem to sense the danger. Cars part before us. It is only seven minutes, but I am constantly looking back over my shoulder to check on Rose. Mei-ling and the nurse are in the back. Mei-ling looks as grey as Rose is now pale blue-purple.

As we pull into the WCH another nurse - a male – is waiting for us. He has a bed on a trolley ready, but they leave it in favour of their feet. He and the practice nurse run off into the hospital carrying Rose, Mei-ling following. I look for somewhere to park the car. I can't find anywhere to park the car. By the time I manage to find a park, I am beside myself. I have no idea where in the hospital they have gone. I guess Accident and Emergency somewhere, but where is that? Which entrance have I come in? Then the practice nurse finds me and takes me to them.

Rose is on an emergency bed, with a full face mask nebuliser. It is ventolin apparently. Mei-ling, amazingly, is smiling at Rose, telling her to breathe, she will be okay. But the ventolin is not working. Rose has some ridiculously low lung capacity. If they cannot get it up, she will die. They switch the nebuliser. Something else. It's adrenalin, they say. Rose is still grey-blue. Her eyes are almost empty. Luckily the adrenalin starts to work. It's croup, they are saying, not asthma. It's croup – as if explaining something helps. But it doesn't help Mei-ling and I. Not until we see the colour start to return to Rose's skin. Now, at least, she is just grey, instead of blue. It can only have been minutes. Rose is starting to breathe again. Mei-ling is still smiling at her. I follow her lead. Here we are, it's okay.

Eventually, Rose stabilises enough for them to remove the oxygen. They are giving her nebulisers regularly, but her lung capacity is back to 60% - 70% - 75%. They want to keep her in for observation. By now it is afternoon. Neither Mei-ling nor I want to leave Rose's side, but they are moving her to a ward now. She will need some things, even if only her glove puppets and bear. Better that she has her own pyjamas, they say. So I will have to go. And then Mei-ling will have to go: she has not even had a shower, and she has her meeting with her Commission that night. I tell her she should cancel, but she refuses.

So I go home first and fetch some of Rose's things. Then, when Rose actually settles into a sleep, I take Mei-ling home and leave her there. I take back a change of clothes for myself, and a soap bag. I plan to wait with her, overnight if necessary. Nurses are great, but I just don't want her to suddenly stop breathing and no-one is there. The hospital is fine with this. I am grateful. But confused now. I had wanted to support Mei-ling. And am wondering, probably irrationally, whether our giant mushroom had anything to do with the sudden onset of Rose's condition. Fungus. Seeds. But the doctor says it is unlikely. Pollen is more likely. Seeds perhaps. But unlikely. Perhaps get it checked. Perhaps, should, likely.

Mei-ling checks in on her way to the Commission meeting. Rose is awake, and eating. Looks in again on her way home. The Commission meeting was a wank. Barnsworth defends the tourism community. Winterbourne defends government. Barrimore defends business concerns about sponsorship risks and the terrorism~tourism backlash. The rest are weak and don't understand their role. She has been given a list of problems to address in management. The message is clear: sack the complainers in order to solve the Commission's problem, and confirm the sound financial future for the company she insists there, including the Next Stage.

I can't bear the thought of Mei-ling going home alone, but she insists she is fine. I sleep on the bed with Rose for much of the night. I watch the nurses come and go, sometimes carrying kidney bowls, sometimes carrying medication or bedding, sometimes just coming back to the nursing station to sit down for a bit. I am glad to be near the nursing station. In the end I sleep too, dreaming uneasily of improbably small seeds falling imperceptibly from veins of our giant mushroom, choking Rose; and am thankfully awake with the first movements on the ward prior to first light.

It's like being on an aeroplane: incubated, life-supported, tired. When Rose wakes, she looks fine. Just fine. She eats a hearty breakfast. And when Mei-ling arrives, she looks fine too. Says I should go home for a rest. But I still can't rest. It's like the day after Rose was born: still running on the adrenalin. Elation. Terror. What's the difference? Hope, I suppose. Present in both, but radically differing in quality in each.

*

Floorboards

Mei-ling really frightened me tonight. I have always thought of her as indomitable, assumed her strength would always be there. Even during her labour with Rose, when she eventually had to give in and admit: I think I am going to need some help, I don't think I can do this anymore – it was still a strong act. After Rose came along, everyone assumed she would dutifully become part of the 'weaker sex', thought it would be an opportunity to patronise her a little more, give them reason make concessions.

But Rose's involvement in her life seems to have made her all the stronger. And through the last six months, she has refused to buy into the various narratives offered her. Even down to the Commission ultimatum: she knows it is the Commission who have created a problem for themselves, that they have subsumed her role and then asked her to resume it again in order to get rid of the problem they have created for themselves.

But Mei-ling has refused to change the way she leads. Refuses to be them. She continues to give Phillipa instructions, but now keeps a record of every one, and follows up every one to a timeline she has specified. So that Phillipa has no option but to produce the figures and cost projections Mei-ling requests, and understands that every excuse for failure to perform is being carefully recorded, even though Mei-ling does not threaten her with the formality of a performance review.

Driffield and McAvaddy are treated in the same way: given clear instruction with precise performance outcomes, and then held to them. But without threat or malice. Mei-ling will produce the management forecasts the Commission has requested, but will not solve for them the management problem they have created.

This takes extraordinary courage. It is something really small and insignificant that tips her over the edge. Phillipa has sent her, through the mail, an invoice for the extra night at the Georges Bay back in January – the extra night *she* suggested we have. She must have been planning this even then. Probably even before. I hadn't even opened the letter. Just handed it to Mei-ling, who left it until Rose went to bed.

At first, Mei-ling is furious. What she really can't understand is how Phillipa could go to these lengths. How far back was it that Phillipa had begun working to a government agenda that intended to destroy her? I kept saying it probably wasn't like that. Agendas developed as events unfolded. But she's a *friend*, Mei-ling keeps saying. I can understand so much, but she's a *friend!* I trusted her with my *daughter* for pity's sake.

And by this time, she is crying. Crying so hard that it is knotting her stomach. She is doubling over. I try to comfort her physically, but she just rolls away from me and staggers up the hall, next to Rose's bedroom. Why did it have to be like this? She just wanted it to stop. What had she done wrong? Nothing, I keep telling her. Then why? she keeps saying, why? I don't deserve this. From any of them. I've done everything they wanted. I've done nothing wrong. I want this to stop. I wish I were dead.

At this stage, she is still trying to fight me off, but I won't let her. I can't bear to see her in such despair. No you don't, I keep saying. I love you. Rose loves you. This will pass. It will pass. We will get beyond this. We will.

She cried and cried, and in the end, once she stopped crying, she was unable to catch her breath. I can't breathe, she says. I can't breathe. Oh my god, I can't breathe. And suddenly we are in a different crisis. I try calming her. Make her drink some water. But she remains agitated and short of breath. So I call the doctor. An after hours service, driven to the door. It only took him an hour, but even with the knowledge that the doctor was on the way, it took Mei-ling all of that time for her agitation to subside and her breathing to stabilise. The doctor could still detect the tail end of the condition when he arrived. It's an anxiety attack he said, particularly when he learnt of Mei-ling's circumstances. He gave her some medication which, thankfully, she took while he was here. She's sleeping now. But I'm still shaking inside.

*

Phone

I've just been on the phone with Mei-ling. This is what it must be like working in the media, to be the reporter on the line as the story breaks. Derek Barrimore has just handed Mei-ling her notice of termination of employment. "I think the protocol at times like this is to offer you the opportunity to resign," he said. "I knew I'd delivered all they had asked, apart from sacking the managers," Mei-ling told me. "But I just couldn't summon the presence of mind to re-iterate that. It was so obviously a done deal."

We had known this would come. Mei-ling has already decided she will contest the dismissal. Fortunately, she has a contract that pre-dates the new IR laws, and the lawyer says she is in a strong position.

"I asked him for a moment to consider it. Thought I might buy some time to prepare a statement or something. But he said: consider all you like, but I have a press conference in the next room in five minutes. He is in there now, announcing my resignation. What am I to do?"

It is the first time Mei-ling has actually asked for my advice so directly. Normally I feed advice into a conversation, trying to do so as unnoticeably as possible, so that it seems more like comment or a response than advice. This is the first time I have found her so confounded by the total contrariness of an action that she simply cannot think of an appropriate response.

I told her she didn't need to do anything. The fact that she was not there with him will speak for itself, and any media that have actually turned up will call her for comment. And she should simply tell the truth: that she has not resigned, and she will be contesting the Commission's position. Frankly, she could say, Barrimore was lucky to find her in her office at all. She had only stepped out of production for a moment.

*

There you go. Didn't take five minutes. She told them she had not resigned. Omitted the bit about contesting the decision. And she's probably right to leave that out. The less she says, the stronger her case at this stage. The rest of King are saying enough to sink themselves several times over.

Balanda's been in. So apologetic, according to Mei-ling. "I had no idea things were this bad," he simpers, offering to take the brunt of rehearsals with the talent. But by 'things', of course, he lays blame nowhere and does not indemnify Mei-ling against the eventual ascription of it. Surely, however, he would know what his partner told Commission members about Mei-ling's relationship with some of the BHT staff towards the end. And the circumstances under which Robert Cunningham was placed in a position to source such information in order to relay it. I can't believe I trusted that man. Yet remain petrified still that he will betray me, at Mei-ling's expense. May already have done so. If not him, Hay. If not Hay, Winterbourne. Just at the moment she needs me most. The anonymous caller at the other end of the line.

*

Welfare

The Premier attended the opening of *We're In This Together* tonight. I think everyone was surprised Mei-ling turned up. Kingsbury was there to 'host' Tresgothic. Mei-ling made a point of intervening and welcoming him herself. She pointedly stressed how positive it is that the State Government has continued to support King's Company's diversity project, despite the withdrawal of the last of the federal funding from the Migrant and Ethnic Support Centres, and from the free English language training.

This sounds as if she is praising the State Government, but of course it is the first time the Premier will have realised he is subsidising a federal failure by funding a Kings Company project promoting cultural diversity. He will have to take this up quickly with the relevant Ministers before the media get wind of the fact that a state government is prepared to sink its own funds into a federal government shortfall. Particularly in an environment in which they also appear committed to a major cultural tourism strategy, again in the face of federal government withdrawal of funding for tourism as part of its anti-terrorism campaign.

But Mei-ling looks earnestly at the Premier, all concern. And he smiles and says it is important to do what they can. And by then Barrimore is at her side, followed closely by Winterbourne, then Dingwall. It doesn't take these boys long.

Barnsworth and Plant are there, but hang back on the fringes. Their travel centre chain is up for sale and I really don't think they know where to put themselves. Mostly Japanese and SE Asian custom, but there seems to be a genuine misperception out there that Australia is a breeding ground for terrorism and it's the tourist industry that is responsible for it.

I find it so easy to smile magnificently at the managers. It is the easiest way to express my total contempt for them: smile and say enthusiastically "Good to see you! This is a great turn-out isn't it? Hasn't Mei-ling done a good job with her range of promotional events for this year?"

Cunningham is there. Smile at him too.

He smiles back, but has the good grace to look slightly uncomfortable with it. Alicia looks genuinely guilty, McAvaddy slightly bashful, but Phillipa delivers it right back, as if nothing has happened and we are still the best of friends. She must be insane. Unless, of course, I am.

*

Doors

Mei-ling stays back late often now, prowling from office to office for evidence while the doors still remain open to her. Charnell continues to have access to her diary, and Mei-ling knows this includes now her records of significant events and meetings and communication, stretching right back to when we first spotted Phillipa with Winterbourne in the coffee shop in Westside. And Mei-ling thinks this is fine. She wants them to know what she is recording and preparing. She wants to retain her dignity and transparency. She wants to leave a trail.

But by the same account, she is going through Phillipa's drawers and Charnell's documents and McAvaddy's tray, photocopying documents and putting them back. Collecting her own evidence, as it were. She has uncovered an alternative program that Phillipa had prepared during *South Pacific*, for instance, and faxes from travel agents interstate contracting alternative creative staff for a replacement program, dated between the managers' approach to the Commission and Mei-ling's meeting with them. Faxes from McAvaddy to Kingsbury during the same period, confirming the Next Stage occupancy Kingsbury had arrived at during the 'stakeholder consultation' meeting.

Mei-ling also brings home copies of incidental material, like invitations with acceptances to the opening of *We're In This Together* to Arte De Leon and Byron Wetherall, which she hadn't authorised and which didn't appear on the official guest list. From Driffield, via Charnell. Across De Leon's was scrawled a late apology. Charnell's hand, so a phone call. Delayed in Karachi after a UK tour of the Old Commonwealth, due to cancellation of landing rights to inbound to Australia from known terrorist ports of origin. And attached to Byron Wetherall's acceptance, a further email from his secretary explaining that he had been arrested when a *Visit the Middle East* promotion he was hosting in

188

Melbourne was closed down by police. Management are clearly worried by the politics. So there is some justice in the world.

When this goes to court, King's Company aren't going to have a leg to stand on – certainly not one that involves Phillipa Hay, Kerry Charnell and Tynan McAvaddy. But it means some late night drives for poor old Rose, as I still don't like the idea of Mei-ling catching a taxi from round there.

*

Sofa

Miriam came to tea tonight. Her contract has also been dissolved. She never actually had one in print to sign. Phillipa and Charnell have just prevaricated and put her off until, now, she is told her services will not be required beyond *The Family Room*. She is planning to contest too, but of course although she clearly has a verbal contract, the IR laws are all the employer's way and she will get nowhere. Nevertheless she is determined to give it a go on principle.

She also showed us some hate mail that is circulating. It has been sent to both the Commission and members of King's Company staff – all except the managers, interestingly. It is full of invective condemning Phillipa, but it contains a colour photograph of her I instantly recognised. I went and fetched our copy of it: one of Phillipa and Mei-ling sitting on our sofa here in the lounge at Witherford Street, with Rose in between them, all smiles. I gave a copy of it to Phillipa at the beginning of the year. There are only the two copies.

I have to admit I looked at Mei-ling for a moment; but only a moment. I know she has neither the moral inclination nor, frankly, the time to reduce herself to something as pathetic as this. Which leaves only Phillipa, at least as the source of the photo. You can clearly see the match between our window frame beside Phillipa's head and the one in the photo on the hate mail.

I find it hard to believe that anyone would go to such lengths to fabricate a crisis. There is a real sense of pathology about this. But in me also. The paranoid in me fears she has enlisted Cunningham to help her. She would need, after all, to put some distance between herself and the act.

*

Hallway

I had Jennifer over today, although I think the thesis is sunk at this stage. I had thought the analysis of the management model in action, as a cultural as well as a structural entity, would sustain some change, but the total collapse of the model itself, and influenced by so many contingent factors, becomes a bit of a sociological nightmare. I could be analysing it for years, and so much is now supposition. How am I going to get to interview key informants like Tresgothic, or Dingwall, or Randall Whippet, or Max Kingsbury? Hi, you've just brought about the complete and utter destruction of my partner's professional career, but look I want to be completely objective about this: would you mind explaining.... Just recount the narrative from your own perspective... I can't quite see it somehow.

I was bemoaning my woes to Jennifer, and asked her what she made of the situation. We were out in the back garden with Rose under the mushroom. I was taking some photos , as Rose can stand under it with her arms stretched up and room to spare now. Jennifer still has to bend over. Quite comical really, and we were laughing even as I was complaining. But Jennifer took a beat when I asked her.

Oh, she said, there were all sorts of rumours flying around. Some people think it's all Mei-ling's fault. Some people think she hasn't been given a fair go. Some think she will stay. Some think she has already gone. So I pressed her again: what did *she* think? Again she said it was difficult to tell. So I asked if she thought there was any one driving force behind it: Kingsbury for instance?

No, she said, Kingsbury was only a mover on the surface. An opportunist at heart. This was a Republican Party issue. Bevan Steele has a lot at stake in the future of Tresgothic, as she understood it. I said we had gone to dinner with him, and she said: I know you did. That's why I'm mentioning him.

Apparently Phillipa has more than just a platonic past with Steele, which goes back before our return to King. Jennifer wouldn't say any more, but recounted instead a tale told her by a close friend who was also deeply involved in the Republican Party.

The friend recalled passing through a room at party headquarters not long after the Tresgothic government had succeeded in gaining election after 10 years in opposition. Steele was there with another party aficionado. They were sitting watching a series of news item edited and spliced together from tv footage and, as one notable opposition *or* fallen Republican figure came onto the screen, Steele and his mate turned to each other, winked, clicked their fingers to make a 'gun' pointing at the screen and said, "Got him!"

At another point in the morning – we were back inside but Rose was still making up stories about the magic mushroom fairies –

Jennifer mentioned brightly that she had been to the psychic Phillipa has been seeing. I tried not to betray my surprise but I had always thought Hay was consulting a psychotherapist. Now I came to think about it, I couldn't remember her ever actually specifying the discipline of the therapist she was seeing. Just 'someone'. To 'help'.

I feigned a sort of Yes, Phillipa never talked much about them. What do they do exactly? Apparently it's a she, and she is a bit of a tarot card/astrologer too. Foretold our arrival in King, and the offer Phillipa would get to join King's Company. Jennifer was very impressed. I asked her what she had learned from her consultation, but she said that mutual confidentiality was part of the deal. And yet she'd just revealed what Phillipa revealed to her. Left me feeling vaguely spooked.

I have become interested in an image I see early in the morning through the frosted glass of our front door from what's left of our house's original hallway. It's the shadow of the ornamental top of the latticework veranda doors we had made to stop people at the top of our front steps, before access to the veranda itself. The two top-sides of these doors rise to meet in the middle, forming a bell-shape or a hill. As the sun rises, these fill the front door glass, but lacking in distinction, because they are a shadow, and the glass is frosted.

I'm unsure of the significance of this image. On one hand it reminds me of a bell in a church; and the fretwork has church-like qualities. But it also reminds me of the horst-like geological structures you see depicted in Chinese "mountains and mist" watercolours, and also find off the coast of Malaysia, Thailand and Vietnam. Potentially they are also quite phallic, but that's not what the image means for me at the moment. And then there is its alignment with our giant mushroom through the house and beyond our back door, between which and the sunrise it stands.

I guess it's Steele's association with Malaysia that brings it to mind here. Anyway, I tried to show it to Jennifer in what was left of the morning sun. Not the same effect. Tried talking about the alignment with the mushroom. She got the idea, but was non-committal. And I am somehow mindful that she is primarily Phillipa's friend before she is mine. But therefore appreciate her candour all the more.

And despite the darkening forces of Phillipa Hay's psychic adviser, I find re-assurance in the knowledge that state politics is the prime mover here. It reduces the chances of Cunningham finding any value in exposing me. Although, of course, I will never know. Until it is too late.

*

Back Garden

I was watering the back garden this afternoon. Rose was playing with toys on back veranda. Mei-ling was inside, pouring over boxes of documents she has had delivered home from King's Company. Phillipa comes up driveway, looks around the garden and sees Rose on the veranda at about the same time as she hears her, I think.

She does not see me as I am tucked away in the corner of the lawn, hidden by intervening bushes and the prominence of the mushroom. But I can see her clearly. She says hallo to Rose, and asks what she is doing. Rose says hallo back quite naturally, and tells her. But it is not the effusive joy Phillipa is used to from Rose; when she would arrive to take her out for a Sunday morning swim, for instance.

We have tried to keep a lot of this from Rose, but I have wondered whether she is picking it up anyway. Particularly after her croup attack. She was certainly non-committal to Phillipa over the rail of the veranda.

Then I said hallo to her too, and she noticed me at last. I moved out into the lawn a little more, so that she could see what I was doing. I'm not sure what she was expecting, or why she had come, but it certainly wasn't to find me watering the back garden. She looked unnerved.

I asked her how she was, still watering. Fine, how are you? How do you think? I said. And then, more directly: What do you want, Phillipa?

Oh, nothing, I …. She smiles weakly … just … She looks back down the drive with uncertainty, then back at Rose with a reassuring smile, then to me again … I just had to … See you, she says finally, and leaves. She still looks swarthy and tall, with her characteristic straight back, but there is something lost and childlike about the bob of the head as she goes. But perhaps I am projecting.

*

Roof

They came and took the car away today. It was the first time I think Rose fully understood what was happening. They chose a time they knew Mei-ling was in a meeting in town with lawyers and Barrimore. Rose and I were sitting on the steps when they arrived – McAvaddy and one of the production staff.

194

Mei-ling and I had thought they might leave it with us as part of the settlement. *The Family Room* has done well. They have extended the season by a week, which gives Mei-ling both an extra few days of official 'notice', and further credibility in her case against the company.

But at their last mediation meeting Barrimore thumped the tabled and said: I expected the car keys at today's meeting. The car is company property and should be returned. Mei-ling's lawyer re-iterated that Mei-ling was challenging the legitimacy of her dismissal, but Barrimore thumped the table again, literally stood up, leant across the table and shouted into Mei-ling's face: I want those keys!

Mei-ling's lawyer subsequently advised her not to give them 'minor cause', so I wasn't surprised to see them pull up. McAvaddy tried to be a bit matey with me, and charming to Rose, but I wouldn't have any of it. He said, apologetically, that he guessed I knew why he was here. I said no. So he had to say he had come for the car. That was when I turned to Rose and said: do you remember Mr McAvaddy from Mummy's work, Rose? He's come to take away our car. They've taken mummy's job away from her, and now they've come to take away our car too.

I couldn't help it. A show in front of the bad guys. But why shouldn't they see what I would have to tell her after they had gone anyway? Help them understand just a little better what they are part of, in case there is any doubt in their minds.

Then I handed over the keys and said nothing further. Didn't even get up. McAvaddy looked like he was going to say something vaguely apologetic, but I just looked away, and he went.

And as the car was driven away, Rose cried tiny tears. "I like our car," she said. "I like it too, darling," I said, "but these people aren't very nice, and it's better than they have what they want so that they can get out of our lives. Then we can be happy again, can't we? You, me and mummy."

Rose nodded, and smiled a little at that idea, and we had a cuddle.

Of course the house will be next, if there is no settlement soon. We won't be able to keep up the mortgage.

*

Tristan Malthorpe's body has been discovered in his Melbourne apartment in an apparent suicide. Lethal overdose of alcohol and sleeping pills after several months of observation by the Special Crimes Authority. The news didn't say any more. I'd love to say this was justice again, but it's far too serious for that. He was such a harmless tosser really. Mei-ling was in tears.

*

Law

I was called to the lawyers this evening. Mei-ling would not leave. She was just sitting in the reception area, hands in her lap, in the corner of those nice spacious but straight-backed sofas they have in lawyers' offices. She was waiting for the letter of settlement the Commission's lawyers had promised. After their third round of negotiations this morning. It's come down from an ambit claim for a quarter of a million to what Mei-ling originally wanted – the pay-out of her contract plus removal costs. We know we will be unable to keep the house.

The lawyers keep telling her that the letter is on its way. The opposition firm will fax it through. But Mei-ling will not leave. It has been one delay after another. One block after another. She will not leave without her letter. There is no reason why it cannot be produced. They have had all afternoon, she says. And she will wait.

Helen kindly takes Rose for tea, so that I don't have to take her with me. When I arrive, staff are still clearly flustering around trying to secure the letter. The legal secretary comes and goes from the lawyer's office, and the lawyer comes out to Mei-ling with yet another up-date. Takes me aside to explain how the day has been. Explains that the obduracy of the Commission and their legal representation is unfathomable, but there is nothing she can do about it. They may just have to go the first round in court. The opposition will fold in the end. And they will pay costs. They really don't have a leg to stand on in law.

I sit with Mei-ling for a while. Her face is impassive. She looks at me as if she does not recognise me. Lets me take her hand, but unresponsively. It's as if her mind has temporarily vacated her brain. The office gradually empties. Staff pass us one by one to enter the lift. Lights are turned off. Eventually it is just us and her lawyer, who looks plaintively at me from her office doorway. Even gives me a cabcharge to get home.

I keep telling Mei-ling we have to go now. There is nothing we can do. We have to go. Eventually she looks blankly at me, gets up and heads for the lift without a word. It is not until she sees Rose running towards her down the path from Helen's house that her face lights up, and life returns to her world. I feel so useless. Even as I know, of course, that this is not about me.

197

Wealth

I imagine you already know how this story ends. Obviously these are not all of the entries in my diary over the last couple of years, but I have given titles to each section that reflect the sociology I see in them looking back. I have left the text pretty much intact, in all its intellectual promiscuity. I find my own attitudes not only difficult to disentangle, but also integral to the narrative.

For your interest, Phillipa continued on into a mild bout of megalomania, in which she touted Tynan McAvaddy as the next Creative Director of Kings Company and was hiring creative staff all over the place. Basically, the Commission kept her there as long as necessary for her to take the fall for Mei-ling's departure.

The Commission itself turned over fairly smartly, with Robert Cunningham, Dale Balanda and Max Kingsbury replacing Derek Barrimore, Harold Winterbourne and Daphne Barnsworth as directors. The new Commission undertook a crash course in governance and, as a fillip to the departees (who had in reality done the hard yards for government), Jane Barrimore was made Chair.

The future of the cultural tourism-led arts economy is in tatters as a King's Company strategy. There was talk in the press of a return to the old tourism commission structure. But then there was, and still is other talk in the press of the dismantling of the tourism commission altogether, and of the collapse of the industry.

The Creative Director who actually replaced Mei-ling was Michael Littlewood, a little-known Ranald Whippet bumboy from what was left of the National Tourism Commission. Evidently nobody quite knew what to do with him, and he was one of the original candidates proposed for King's Company by Whippet and Malthorpe at the time of the selection in which Mei-ling was successful.

Once he took over, things went back to the way they were before. Arte de Leon, Byron Wetherall and Lillith Plant got their Associate Director status back; Plant particularly grateful, as she no longer had a business. The promotions in the Performance Centre dropped back to a token showing. The company focus went back to media campaigns and tour packaging, going for the overtly non-terrorist allies like the US and Europe. The Company basically became a retail outlet for promotions by the other struggling state and national tourism commissions, and the local Associate Directors were lucky if they secured one consultancy a year, and little spin-off business.

Meanwhile Hannah and Chamberlain's company secured their own promotional funding from government. Compensation for having their reputation 'smeared' by the police investigation, presumably. Dale Balanda's Cult Tourism, of course, thrived.

In the end it was unclear whether it was government politics or the anti-tourism campaign that brought Mei-ling down. The need for bureaucracy to make even the most outrageous of government policy gaffs real by institutionalising them has more than halved the country's tourism income. The immigration detention camps are now permanently designated for suspect terrorist tourists as well as so-called "illegal" refugees. The Senate Tribunal on the Terrorist Impact of Tourism remains a standing committee of government, and regional Australia has fallen further into decline as one more revival strategy suffers at the hands of government ineptitude. All that's left to coastal Australia outside the cities is the retirees, as the tourist industry collapses into the disinterest of the major tourist supply countries. Except in one small region of New South Wales, which I will turn to shortly.

There was an interview in the local daily with Littlewood early on in which he religiously avoided ascribing any blame whatsoever to Mei Ling for the King's Company's subsequent failings. The journalist, of course, had no such compunctions. Mei-lings actual achievements with King's Company never saw the light of day. For a while I sent them around to leading media outlets and journalists, but in the end I ran out of anger. Nobody was interested. The story they thought would sell advertising had already been told.

Mei-ling remained strong right up until the last, I believe. She was certainly determined to see her unfair dismissal case through, despite the inhuman tactics deployed by the company and its lawyers. I know she remained committed to seeing so much of it as a learning experience. What tipped her over, I think, was being presented with a photo of Rose during the first public hearing.

The defence were trying to discredit her, predictably, and they produced the hate mail Phillipa (it can only have been Phillipa) had circulated about herself. Then they produced the photograph I had given Phillipa, of she and Mei-ling sitting on our sofa in Witherford Street, Rose in between them. They asked Mei-ling if she recognised the photo, and who had taken it. And Mei-ling started to cry. "I would never write this sort of thing," she said, "And I do not support or condone it in any way."

That was all she said. She cried all that night, once Rose was in bed. And she played with Rose most of the next day. That night she held our original of the photo most of the night. I couldn't draw her out. I kept saying the usual things: she knew it wasn't her, she must realise it is not her fault, they are just objectifying her, this was classic scapegoating, there is nothing more she could have done, she did all of the right things, we had talked this through thoroughly and we knew it was a sound strategy, the fault lies elsewhere, this will pass, etc.

In the end she said that she understood all of that, and she didn't even mind that they tried to implicate me, as the photographer. It was the fact they had drawn Rose into it that she couldn't abide. She knew that ultimately she was responsible for our situation, and she could live with that, but the one thing she had always thought she could do was protect Rose. And in the end, she realised even this was not possible. Those who required her scapegoating were unable to stop at the deconstruction of her entire professional life. And to do that, they believed they had to destroy her personally as well. She was so matter-of-fact, but the tears just ran and ran down her face. There was nothing I could say.

I suggested we all went out together in the morning. Just to a park or something simple, that Rose would enjoy. She said yes, that would be nice. And we went to bed, and cuddled. It took me a while to get to sleep. I was worried this was just the beginning. If Hay and McAvaddy had my affair with Robert Cunningham up their sleeve, now was just the time for them to use it. In court. The photo and who took it was just a pot-boiler.

It was still dark when I awoke, and at first I thought Mei-ling had just gone to the loo. After a while I went and checked, and it was clear she was not in the house. I checked outside, and she was nowhere to be found. I thought then that perhaps she had gone out for a walk, to clear her mind. At that stage, I didn't realise the extent to which she had internalised what she was saying: that our situation as a family was her fault.

By lunchtime, however, I was beside myself. I couldn't ring Jennifer; she was too bound up in the pathology. So I rang Helen and Sharon instead, and they were great. We had the police around by tea time, and while they were full of re-assurances about people turning up, they certainly acted quickly enough taking down statements and details and getting out an alert.

After that, I talked myself steadily into a state of quiet panic. I expected Mei Ling to turn up. Spent hours and hours while Rose was in kindy wandering around the Cultural Centre, and the places we used to go, expecting to find her at any minute. But then I began to find the little hoards of money in 'secret' places around the house, and realised this had been building with Mei-ling, along with a paranoia, for some time.

Even so, I hoped it was something she had gone away to 'get over' or 'work through', and she would return to us 'recovered'. I became terrified she would return to Witherford Street when I was not there.

The police knew what had happened, of course. They ran the scenario past me on Day Two, because they had a reported sighting from the shop owner. I dismissed it out of hand, and promptly buried it in some deep, inaccessible part of my brain. Mei-ling would never buy a gun. Suicide was out of the question. She loved Rose too much. But by the same account I imagined a man out walking his dog who finds her remains months later, in a serious state of decomposition. But her purse (with ID) is still on her, and she is wearing the moonstone necklace Rose and I bought for her last birthday.

Piecing her movements together, police believed Mei-ling had caught the first train of the day from the city to the end of the line, walked up the road to a gun shop she obviously knew was there, and bought herself a .22 and a gun licence giving a false address from out of town. Their records will show that she walked another

3 kilometres into a secluded patch of bush she must also have looked out on a mapThe trail ended there.

I'm sure you can imagine the rest of the scenario. How much I howled and ranted and raved and blamed and blamed and blamed at this prospect. But in the end I knew in my heart that she would have done it because it was the only way she could see of protecting Rose, by removing herself from the picture. I think if you truly love someone, you *will* do anything for them. At least, Mei-ling did.

And then the funeral – or a 'ceremony of remembrance', as the Lees would term it. Not even a celebration of her life. For them, it would be like the second burial the Chinese have, after time in the *gam tap* up on the hill in the geomantically appropriate spot for the bones to wait, in their sealed earthenware urn, for the right permanent site to be found by the *feng shui* man. Mei-ling would be, by that time, certainly a well-seasoned assortment of bones.

And of course no-one from "the profession" would come. Just Jennifer, and of course Robert Cunningham to rub it in. Comforting Jennifer his self-appointed role for the day.

Cunningham finds a way of cornering me outside the chapel, with his best solicitudinous affect, much though I try to avoid eye contact. I expect him to tell me how sorry he is, how much Mei-ling will be missed, how much he has respected her, and any number of other platitudes. But instead he says, quite directly, "I never told anyone, you know. She wouldn't have found out from me."

And then of course I cry. Uncontrollably. So much guilt. So much worry. All bound up together. I even let him hold me. But after a time, when I disengage, thinking of Rose, wondering where she is, he doesn't attempt to re-engage. He waves a loose "See you" and leaves with Jennifer. And Rose re-appears with the Lees.

I remain unable to come at a conspiracy theory. In fact by this time I have given up on theories altogether. I can never find one that explains the all-pervading agency played by culture in the action of power throughout Mei-ling's experience in King. All of her evidence remains around us here in Withington Street in unopened, carefully ordered and marked archive boxes. And now, nowhere for it to become manifest in terms of rightful retribution. Mei-ling has just slipped through the gaps between so many in whose interests she was not. The net of culture, which saves so many of us, failed to save her. Hers is a convenient death. Not even a tourist in her own profession.

*

As you can see, I have become the author of the narrative in which I play a part. In the days following Mei Ling's disappearance I fall into a chasm between disbelief and its suspension. Meaning for me becomes lost as soon as it is found by my questing being. I am living proof of the French Post-structuralist philosopher Jacques Derrida's 'trace'. By the time the word is even formed, meaning has moved on. I lose my sense of self, must manufacture narrative in order to hold my mind from despair. You must question everything I write. For I am no author here, just the subject of my own story, the sole survivor of myself.

Looking back from this distance, however, I still believe what I thought in those days: that there is a pathology at the heart of patriarchy that infects even women with the best will in the world. And it's a pathology that only men will be able to cure, and will have to cure if we are to survive as human beings. I thought I had seen my house pulled apart around me such that the planks and beams and cladding and boards I had painstakingly pieced together flew out in one action into a space I did not understand, never to be seen again.

And in reality, when Rose came to me in the mornings towards the end of that first week, able now to climb out of her bed, saying "Mummy home," I groaned internally and clung to my daughter, imagining her disbelief in the immanence of such grief, ever hopeful of reprieve.

It was not until the seventh morning, which was a Sunday, that I awoke to the realisation that Rose had not awoken me. Leapt out of bed with concern to check her bedroom, and find her gone. Moved through the house with increasing panic. Noticing the back door onto the verandah open – HOW could she have opened it? Rushing through hoping to find her playing in the spare room, or on the verandah, or in the . . .

To see her sitting under the mushroom with Mei Ling, reading a book together.

In just seven days, my daughter had taught me faith. And trust.

*

"I really did intend to do it," Mei Ling was struggling through tears. "I felt such a failure. A coward."

"I'm glad you didn't," I sniveled, equally overcome with both relief and vestigial grief.

Rose was down for her nap. Mei Ling and I finally had the chance to share what had transpired. She had only been away for two days. The rest of the week she had been stalking the house, not quite sure how to return in her shame.

"How could you ever think that of me," I sobbed. "I love you. We both do."

Mei Ling shook her head. "I was not well David. Not well at all. I am still not well."

I hugged her again.

"Did you…" I tried to ask, but choked on the question.

Mei Ling withdrew from our embrace and made me face her.

"I sat down to do it, David. I did that. But I couldn't stop thinking of Rose. And how I couldn't do this to her. Or to you. But mostly her. I guessed about Robert, David. I did not care, but was angry with you nevertheless. For not being where you could have been. For not being with me. But Rose…"

The tears welled up in her eyes again, but she did not avert her gaze.

"I took the bolt out of the rifle, and removed the ammunition clip. I left the rifle there, in the bush, and dropped the bolt and clip into separate bins on a long walk back to the railway station."

"I was not well, but I could not kill myself."

*

The rest is, as they say, history. Once word got to King's Company that Mei Ling had "disappeared" and then returned, the company settled out of court almost immediately. I doubt they fancied how it would look in the next hearing: Tourist Commission drive CEO to suicide attempt.

Nevertheless we chose not to witter away the rest of Mei Ling's contract (which she was all she got, but also all she wanted) on interest payments to the bank. We put the house on the market, planning to move into rental in Westside and work out where to next.

The real estate publicity made much of the mushroom in the back garden. The image was so popular we achieved prime advertising space in real estate hostings with large ads we didn't have to pay for, they commanded such attention. People attended the open inspections just to marvel.

It was ironic that, the night before auction, thieves stole it. We woke up to find traces of broken mushroom husk littering our garden, and strewn along the side driveway out onto the street. They must have made such a mess of the thing. Heaven knows what they wanted it for – proportions of the stolen property, however presented, would be obvious to all.

I joked with Mei Ling that it was probably Philippa. If she couldn't have our daughter, or Mei Ling's day in court, she would certainly have our family giant mushroom.

The auctioneer made great fun out of the theft, showing its photograph to the assembled crowd, and then extolling them: "Believe us, it *was there yesterday!* This is no hoax. There are giant mushroom thieves afoot! Do guard yours carefully!"

The upbeat atmosphere worked for us – it was like being at a party – and we sold well above the falling prices around East King.

Ironically, before we even settled on the sale, Mei Lin applied for a job running a Community Theatre Company in Wagga Wagga, down in southern New South Wales. I was concerned that this was a manic manifestation of a bipolar cycle. I was still worried about her mental health. After all we had said about the performing arts and their highest point of consciousness!

But I should have trusted my darling's intelligence of feeling.

"David, what do you think are the chances of them even interviewing me? This is so far outside my experience, but maybe they mean it when they say they want to increase cultural tourism as an outcome of their theatre company's activity? What do I lose?"

And they did interview her – by phone. I sat listening – she was magnificent on the community development benefits of a cultural tourism focus for the theatre company, in addition to its existing local culture impact.

And when they asked her about her theatre skills:

"My friends, I have produced cultural tourism productions which involve professional performers, live musicians, local volunteer performers, giant puppetry, audio-visual extravaganzas, that have occupied and engaged entire towns for an entire day. What do you want?"

And so it was that Mei Ling Lee became a niche Community Theatre Director and (a contractual requirement on which she insisted) CEO of what she rapidly renamed the Murrumbidgee Community Performing Group.

It was like a rebirthing for my professionally broken love. A garden in which she could flourish according to her nature.

All that she did worked superbly. It was like the old days. Before, with a bit of restructuring, my Masters eventually came through, I got a job in the local Council as a Community Development Officer, and was thus able to work hand in glove with Mei Ling. Between us, we resurrected the local agricultural show as the basis for a whole of community re-enactment of the region's substantial past, using professional performers to anchor key roles, circus and puppetry.

From this basis Mei Ling developed satellite performance pieces about contemporary issues – the struggle of the women's shelter to get itself established, the enthusiasm but pitfalls with which the town embraced its role as regional recipient for refugee immigrants, the four State battle for water from the mighty Murray-Darling system, the scurrilous antics of local bushranger Ben Burrows, and many more.

The "Wagga Wake-up" became a national drawcard for enthusiasts in the performing arts, tourism, and those just seeking a taste of a rural life they'd learnt about at school, in the context of the gourmet food and wine experiences and city-quality entertainment.

It wasn't long before the annual event was featuring the Sydney Symphony Orchestra under the stars at a local winery, and ended with Australia's first and, later, foremost country-meets-city music festival. And of course there were laserscapes throughout the town, and fireworks every night.

The event not only brought big dollars into the town and paid for itself many times over, it also served as a marketing platform for the local program of Murrumbidgee Community Performing Group's activity, and other cultural events throughout the year as well, as Come Back Again discounts to encourage return business.

Tourism in the region later benefited further from our Do The Drive campaign, heralding Wagga as *the* overnight stop for the drive everyone had to do at least once in their lifetime. (We never really specified whether it was Melbourne to Sydney, Sydney to Adelaide, or Brisbane to Perth. We just tried to grab them all, and trebled our overnight stay rate.)

Once I became Council's Business Manager, and Mei Ling scored as seat on Council, we were really able to maximize and demonstrate the economic as well as cultural benefits to the region. Nowadays, other rural and regional councils visit on benchmarking expeditions. Academics come to study what we have achieved. And we cooperate with them all assiduously. But we never reveal our secret: which is, of course, Rose.

The privilege and joy of being part of our daughter's growth has never ceased to amaze us. We were the unashamedly doting parents attending her choir performances in primary school. We clapped unstintingly through her high school forays into drama, dance and the school orchestra. And Mei Ling took such pleasure in creating events in which Rose could participate as part of our professional activity. Rose grew such a love for the arts, but also for life in and around the country. And Mei Ling never looked back.

I sang the praises of accountancy as a career for years, but we always knew it was a joke. When she started off studying performing arts at the local Charles Sturt University, where her mum taught master classes when she could, we thought our luck was in. But eventually the lure of the sandstone and fifties universities in Sydney won out.

These days she has a boyfriend in Sydney studying environmental design. We secretly hope if the relationship becomes serious he will develop a career-building interest in Wagga, but we know there is no stopping our girl. Who is, in reality, a woman now☺.

And I did learn to play with Rose. I found we could share a sense of humour. And engaging in it has been a source of joy and fun for me ever since, and binds us to this day. And I have surrendered that sense of 'other' in which I sought to cast myself in relation to Mei-ling even in the act of trying to transform my role as father and man. Given up life roles such as 'supporter; and 'advisor' and 'facilitator'. Mei-ling and I just have relationship, in which love deepens every day. Practice for us exceeds the superficial boundaries of work, leisure and gender. We have too much to value and enjoy in our lives together.

I still believe that, as men, it is we who need to change ourselves if we are to free human existence from the ineluctable destructiveness and violence of patriarchal thinking and behaviour. And am now personally much more at peace with myself, at such distance in time, geography and experience from the internecine cultural vortices of King. If anything, it is a shame that I discovered my bisexuality in a context that politicised it with a pervading climate of betrayal, deceit, and small-mindedness.

I could construe my one sexual act with a man as a symptom of the increasing cultural trauma in which I was finding myself embroiled at the time. But the truth is I enjoy the freedom I now have to find men potentially an object of desire and love. And I seem to see so many more men now openly loving their children, loving their partners, whatever the gender. It gives me hope that we are capable of the transformation so very much needed of us if we are to help make this world a habitable place for people to share in society.

One fact remains irksome, however; like a claw lodged in my mental matter: why did the police never tell me they'd found the disassembled rifle?

* * *

THE END

* * *